A Hot Montana Summer

A Hot Montana Summer

A Glacier Creek Romance

Karen Foley

A Hot Montana Summer

Tule Publishing First Printing, March 2018

The Tule Publishing Group, LLC

First Publication by Tule Publishing Group 2018

ISBN: 978-1-948342-78-0

Prologue

"YOU'RE GOING TO marry me someday."

Rachel McCafferty spun around from the sink where she was mixing a pitcher of lemonade to stare at the boy sitting on the far side of the kitchen island. He watched her with solemn blue eyes, and his narrow face gave no indication he was joking.

Rachel smiled uncertainly. She didn't want to crush the kid's ego, but neither did she want to give him any false hope. He was, after all, just a kid. He had about as much chance of marrying her as a snowball had of surviving ten minutes in Hell. So why, then, did the expression in his eyes—unwavering and intense—cause such an odd tightening sensation in her chest? Abruptly, she turned her back to him. Reaching up, she took two glasses down from the cupboard.

"Well," she finally responded, eyeing him cautiously as she poured a glass of lemonade and slid it across the countertop to him, "seeing as you're only twelve years old, you're expecting me to wait an awfully long time, aren't you?"

"Fourteen."

Rachel set the pitcher down on the counter with a grin. "Fourteen years? I'll be an old maid by then!"

"No," he said quietly. "I'm not twelve. I'm actually fourteen. At least," he amended, with a shrug, "I will be in another month. But since you mentioned it, I'm pretty sure in fourteen years, you and I *will* be married."

Rachel stared at Jamie Colter, too taken aback by his brash confidence to know how to respond. He was small for his age, and skinny. His family had lived across the street for as long as Rachel could remember, and he and her younger brother, Dylan, had been best buds practically from the time they could walk. Jamie was almost a permanent fixture at their house, but Rachel paid about as much attention to him as she would any other piece of furniture. Still, he seemed like a nice kid, and the last thing she wanted was to hurt his feelings.

"Jamie," she finally said, choosing her words carefully, "I'm flattered, I really am, but I'm sure in a couple of years—no, a couple of *weeks*—you're going to forget all about me."

"I won't."

"I'm twenty years old, Jamie. I'm almost done with college." She slanted him a skeptical look. "No offense, but you haven't even started high school yet."

Jamie didn't say anything. He picked up his glass and took a long swallow of lemonade, his eyes never leaving hers.

"Besides," Rachel continued, keeping her tone light, "once school starts in the fall, you're going to have so many pretty girls your own age to choose from, you won't want anything to do with me."

Jamie set his glass down and carefully wiped his mouth. "It won't matter how many other girls I date between now and then. It'll just be practice for the real thing."

Rachel gave a bark of surprised laughter. "Jamie Colter! You're unbelievable."

"Who's unbelievable? And how long have you been here, Jamie? Why didn't you come upstairs and get me?" Dylan McCafferty's tone was mildly annoyed as he slid onto a stool beside Jamie and reached for Rachel's untouched glass of lemonade. "I told Lucas we'd meet him at the skate park to try out your new board."

"Yeah, well, I stopped to talk with Rachel."

Dylan's face twisted in bemusement. "*Why?*"

Jamie grinned. "Because I like talking to her."

Dylan snorted in disgust. "That's only because you don't live with her. Trust me, if she was your sister, you wouldn't want anything to do with her."

Sliding from the stool, Jamie scooped his skateboard up from where it leaned against the island and tucked it under his arm. "Which is why," he said, slanting a wicked grin at Rachel, "I thank God every day she's not *my* sister."

Chapter One

Twelve Years Later

JAMIE LEANED HEAVILY on his crutches as he thumbed through the mail, enjoying the morning sun on his shoulders and the dewy coolness of the grass beneath his bare feet. After a year in the Syrian Desert, he didn't think he'd ever grow tired of the crisp mountain air and deep, cool forests that characterized his hometown of Glacier Creek, Montana.

"Honey, you should put some clothes on! It's not that warm out."

Glancing up, Jamie saw his mother standing in the open doorway of the single-story, ranch-style house where he'd grown up. A tall, attractive woman in her fifties, she was dressed for her morning Zumba class in a pair of yoga pants and a bright pink hoodie. In contrast, he wore only a pair of shorts. Getting a pair of jeans to fit over his leg cast was impossible, and he hadn't yet gotten around to putting on a shirt. The day promised to be warm and dry, so maybe he'd just lounge in the backyard, like he'd done almost every day since he'd come home.

"I'm fine, Mom," he said.

"Your breakfast is ready," she called, crossing the front yard to the driveway. "I'm leaving now, so don't let it get cold. And be careful! You don't want to do too much. You'll exhaust yourself and fall, and I won't be here to help you."

Jamie raised his hand in farewell as she backed her car onto the street, and drove away. He sighed and closed the mailbox. He'd been home for almost two months, and as his injuries healed and he grew stronger, the walls of his childhood home closed in more tightly around him. His mother worried and fussed over him like he was still a child. His dad had explained to him the fear and anxiety she'd experienced when they'd learned he'd been injured in Syria, but Jamie wished she'd relax, just a little. He was home now, however reluctantly.

Thank God they were leaving in a couple of days for their annual cruise with the McCaffertys. This year they were cruising through the Hawaiian Islands for two weeks. His mother had wanted to cancel the trip, insisting he couldn't be left alone, but Jamie and his dad had convinced her he would be fine. He was twenty-six years old, and had been taking care of himself for almost eight years. Knowing his mother, she'd make sure the cupboards and fridge were stocked with enough food and beer to last him a month. She'd probably already contacted the neighbors and put them on notice to provide assistance while she was gone, just in case.

He sighed and scrubbed a hand over his face. He loved Glacier Creek, but there wasn't a whole lot going on in the way of excitement. Even hanging out with his old high school buddies at The Drop Zone, one of his favorite pubs, was a major undertaking. The leg cast, which extended from his toes to mid-thigh on his right leg, made it impossible to drive, so he was pretty much at the mercy of his parents if he wanted to go out anywhere. They'd only be gone for two weeks, but Jamie would be housebound for the duration. He could already feel the itch of cabin fever crawling across his skin.

He glanced at the house across the street, and the empty driveway. Even his best friend, Dylan, who had joined the local smoke jumper crew as a wildland firefighter, was off battling a blaze somewhere in Idaho. Jamie hadn't seen him in a couple of years, but decided as soon as Dylan returned, he'd get back in touch with him.

As teenagers, they'd sworn one day they would start their own extreme adventure company, along with their third friend, Lucas Talbot. There was nothing they had enjoyed more than pushing themselves to the limit. As adults, they'd each found a career doing just that, but in ways they hadn't imagined when they'd been kids. He missed Dylan and Lucas. Too much time had passed since the three of them had been together.

His thoughts turned briefly to Dylan's sister, Rachel, as they always did when he looked at the McCafferty house.

Man, he'd been crazy about her as a kid, but time and biology had conspired against him. Seven years his senior, she hadn't been remotely interested in a scrawny, prepubescent boy. By the time he'd grown up, filled out, and became a man, she'd found herself some rich playboy named Deke Narducci, aka the Deke-wad, and married him.

And that had been that.

He'd been out of the running before he'd even had a chance to compete.

Jamie hadn't seen Rachel in years, which was probably for the best. She'd been his first serious crush. He still experienced a bittersweet pang of longing and regret whenever he thought of her. She'd been so beautiful, so confident, and so energetic in everything she'd done, that watching her had been like staring too long at the sun. She'd dazzled him. Whenever she'd come home from college, Jamie had found a reason to spend more time at the McCafferty house than he did his own. Dylan had been disgusted by Jamie's obvious infatuation with Rachel, and teased him mercilessly. Jamie hadn't cared. The abuse had been worth the reward of seeing Rachel, of simply circling in her orbit. She'd been so full of life, big dreams, and big plans that he'd been in awe of her.

Tucking the bundle of mail into the waistband of his shorts, Jamie adjusted his crutches and turned to go back into the house, when a car turned onto the street. He wouldn't have paused to watch except it was a sweet little Porsche Carrera GT in a gleaming shade of silver. Low-slung and sexy as hell, Jamie would have given his left nut to take it for a spin. Even as he wondered why a sleek set of wheels like that would have any business driving down Pinewood Avenue, it turned into the McCafferty driveway.

Jamie's mouth nearly fell open. Had Dylan's dad finally succumbed to a midlife crisis? A car like that was easily worth six figures. Unable to resist, he swung his crutches in the direction of the car, and then stopped short as the driver's door opened, and a woman climbed out.

Holy shit.

There was no mistaking the shiny swish of dark hair, or the sweetly curved ass beneath the snug white shorts. Jamie stopped breathing.

Rachel.

She hadn't changed much in the three years since he'd last seen her, except she was even sexier than he remembered. Admittedly, the encounter at a popular L.A. restaurant had been so brief and unexpected, she hadn't even seen him. But Jamie had recognized her. More importantly, he'd recognized the man who'd been aggressively hitting on a pretty brunette near the restaurant bar, while Rachel had sat at an outdoor dining table waiting for him to return with their drinks. She'd always had terrible taste in guys, as evidenced by her choice of husband.

Jamie had thought about that night so many times over the last few years, and still regretted he hadn't gone over to say hello to Rachel. Or better yet, outed her dirtball spouse.

In his fantasy, Rachel always slapped Deke hard across the face and declared their marriage was over. Then she ran, teary-eyed, from the restaurant. That's where he came in, offering a strong shoulder for her to lean on. The fantasy always ended with the two of them in his bed.

She hadn't yet spotted him standing in the middle of the street, staring at her like an idiot, and for a moment Jamie thought about turning tail and running. Only there was no running in his current condition. There was only painstakingly slow, snail-like progress. But he didn't want her to see him like this, looking so fucking pathetic. Maybe, if he stood perfectly still, she wouldn't notice him. Or maybe he could turn away and if she did happen to look in his direction, she wouldn't recognize him. He was about to do that when her gaze swung toward him, and their eyes locked. He saw the precise instant when recognition caused her eyes to widen, and then sweep over him. Her mouth formed a wordless *oh*.

He smiled, feeling as if he'd been caught doing something naughty. "Hey, Rachel. Long time, no see."

"Yeah," she responded, sounding a little stunned. "Jamie, right? Wow. I would never have guessed. You look...great." Her expression immediately turned contrite. "I mean, except for the leg. What happened?"

Jamie shrugged. "A mortar attack in Syria, and I was trapped beneath some debris. No biggie."

No biggie. He sounded like a complete moron, and for the first time in his life, he couldn't wait to get away from

Rachel McCafferty. He wasn't prepared to see her, and was definitely not ready to talk to her. She'd caught him completely off guard. She was even prettier than he remembered, and it was all he could do not to stare, bug-eyed, at her. He had an impression of slim, bare legs and a silky top that clung to her curves. She was so freaking beautiful, it hurt to look at her. He quickly looked away. It seemed some things never changed, like whenever she was near his brain stopped synapsing.

Now she looked uncomfortable, as if she didn't know what to say, either. If she followed the news, she'd know the attack on the Marine compound five months earlier had been deadly. He'd lost two buddies that night, and had been trapped beneath the rubble for an agonizing eighteen hours before he'd been rescued. He'd been lucky; his injuries had been extensive, but not life-threatening.

"How long are you home for?" he asked, ignoring the warning bells jangling in his head, telling him to just let her go. Because what was the point in small talk? She'd married some dude on the East Coast, and that was that. The guy was a total dick, but Rachel had hitched her wagon to his horse. Or at least to his little Porsche Carrera.

"I'm not sure." She shrugged, looking both uncomfortable, and something else. Angry? "A while," she finally said. "At least until I find my own place."

Jamie's antennae went up, and he sharpened his gaze on her. "Oh, yeah? You moving back here?"

She looked away for a moment, and cleared her throat. Jamie had the distinct sense she was struggling to compose herself. When she turned back to look at him, there was no mistaking the sheen of tears in her dark eyes, and she swiped at them with her fingertips.

"Yes."

"Hey," he said, frowning at her distress. He'd never seen Rachel cry. He moved closer, until he was in her driveway. "Are you okay? Did something happen?"

She gave a bitter laugh. "You could say that. Deke and I just got divorced. Like literally, just a few days ago." She flapped a hand. "I mean, we haven't lived together for almost two years, but the papers just came through the other day, and I don't know…it just seems so *final.* The end of a chapter." She drew in a deep breath and expelled it. "I had to get away, so here I am."

Something shifted in Jamie's chest, and then broke loose and began turning cartwheels of unadulterated delight.

Divorced.

As in…no longer married.

Available.

"About damned time," he said, unable to disguise his satisfaction. "That guy was a douche, and the only one who couldn't see it was you."

Rachel's face registered shock, and then affront. "I beg your pardon, but I wasn't aware you ever met Deke."

"I did, actually. A couple of times. Once when the two of

you came home for a visit, and once out in L.A., at a restaurant called The Point."

Rachel tipped her head, considering. At least she no longer looked like she might burst into tears, for which Jamie was grateful. He could handle just about anything except a woman's tears.

"We were only at The Point once, a few years ago," she finally said. "You were there? Why didn't you say hello?"

"I was with a bunch of guys from my unit, and it didn't seem like the right time," he hedged. "You probably wouldn't have recognized me, anyway."

Her eyes swept over him again, and this time he could have sworn there was something else in her eyes...a feminine awareness and maybe even appreciation. It was all Jamie could do not to puff himself up beneath her gaze. He forced himself to lean easily on his crutches and act as if it were no big deal to be standing there, talking to her.

"Probably not," she finally agreed. "You've, ah, changed a lot."

"Damn straight. I'm not fourteen anymore."

Her eyes flicked over him again and he watched with interest as warm color crept up her neck, before washing into her cheeks.

"No, you're certainly not," she agreed.

The undisguised approval in her tone was so clear, Jamie started to blush. He cast around desperately for a safer topic.

"That's an impressive set of wheels," he said, indicating

the car. "Is it a celebration gift to yourself, or the spoils of war?"

Rachel glanced at the silver sports car, and her mouth curved in a rueful smile. "Deke gave me the car just before we split—it was supposed to be a birthday gift, but in retrospect I think it was actually a guilt-gift. Anyway, we have a house—*had* a house—in Jackson Hole. We kept the car there, so when I flew into Wyoming yesterday, I picked it up. I spent last night in Bozeman, and drove the rest of the way this morning."

A home in Jackson Hole.

A Porsche Carrera.

Jamie felt a little stunned. He knew Deke Narducci was wealthy; he was heir to the Narducci shipping and cruise lines, after all, but he hadn't given much thought to just how filthy rich the guy really was. Deke was mostly famous for hanging out with other famous people on his luxury yacht, or for being seen at popular celebrity events, or vacationing in exotic locales. Jamie had always written him off as an entitled playboy. But seeing evidence of his lavish lifestyle—one Rachel had shared—made him realize they came from completely different worlds. He couldn't begin to compete.

"Did I say something wrong?"

Jamie jerked his attention back to Rachel, who studied him with a small frown. He shook his head. "Nah. I was just thinking it must be hard coming back to this, after what you've been used to with Deke."

Rachel looked around, as if seeing the neighborhood for the first time. "Actually," she said, "it feels really good. I'd forgotten how green everything is, and how good the air smells. I've missed being home."

"So you're not going back to New York?"

"Maybe just to clear out my apartment, but I don't think I'll live there again."

Jamie tried to contain his grin, and failed.

She stared at him as if mesmerized, then made a vague gesture toward the house with one hand. "I should probably go in, say hello to my parents, you know…get settled."

Jamie nodded. "Right. I should get back, too. It was great seeing you, Rachel."

"Yes," she agreed. "We should do it again soon." Realizing what she said, she shook her head and gave an embarrassed laugh. "I mean, I hope to see you again soon." Clearly flustered, she gave him a quick smile. But before she turned away, she gave him one last, all-encompassing look, as if she couldn't quite help herself. This time, there was no mistaking the admiration in her eyes, before she abruptly spun away and all but ran into the house.

And just like that, Jamie was back in the game.

He swung his crutches in the direction of his parents' house, amazed at how, in the space of mere minutes, the town of Glacier Creek had just gotten a whole lot more exciting.

Chapter Two

RACHEL STOOD AT the window of the first-floor guest bedroom and stared across the street at the Colter house, but Jamie was nowhere to be seen. Disgusted with herself for even looking, she turned away. She was acting like a smitten teenager, but she couldn't stop thinking about their earlier encounter. Had that muscular slab of sexiness really been skinny little Jamie Colter? She pictured again the broad shoulders and washboard abs, and the biceps that looked as if he could easily bench press a small car. She'd noted the new, raw scar on his abdomen that had disappeared beneath the waistband of his shorts. The only things that hadn't changed about Jamie Colter were his blue eyes and his audacious grin.

She recalled again how he had looked at her. She'd registered the surprise in his expression, but hadn't expected the blatantly masculine perusal that had followed, or her own improbable reaction. She'd blushed like a schoolgirl, and the heat of his gaze on her skin had been like a palpable caress. She'd been celibate for way too long if she was fantasizing about a guy she hadn't seen since he was a scrawny teenager, and was way too young for her even if she was interested.

Which she wasn't.

Definitely not.

She knew all about younger men, having been married to one for five years. Well, three years if she wanted to get technical. They hadn't lived together for the last two years of the marriage.

Just thinking about Deke made her hands close into fists. How had their marriage gone so wrong? In the beginning, it had seemed like the stuff of fairy tales, and he'd made her feel like a princess. He'd given her everything, denied her nothing.

Rachel had been part of a team of professionals, hired by Deke to manage every aspect of his privileged life. But after just a few days in his company, he'd made it clear he wanted her. He'd pursued her with a single-minded determination that didn't end, even after he'd left New York. No one could blame her for being swept up in the romance of it all.

Deke had been so wonderful, so charming, so intent on making her happy. And he had. Not just with the extravagant gestures and gifts he'd lavished on her, but with his full and undivided attention, as if the sun rose and set on her.

When Elite Concierge Services had finally let her go, stating she had violated company rules by becoming involved with a client, Deke had promised to make it right. He'd flown her to the Maldives for two weeks, where he'd asked her to marry him, despite the fact they'd only been dating for six weeks.

It hadn't mattered that he was only twenty-five to her twenty-eight. They'd had so much fun together, and his energy had been boundless. Despite the fact his family claimed she was only interested in his money, Rachel had found Deke's charm and humor to be his most appealing attributes. Why else would she have signed the prenup? She just hadn't realized he was more interested in the chase than he was in the relationship.

Once they were actually married, his interest had quickly waned. Deke had started to travel without her, telling her she'd be happier remaining at home. Only they hadn't had a home, not really. Deke had owned houses and apartments all over the world, but none of them had felt like home. As he'd traveled—to movie premieres, parties, and lavish fundraisers—she'd remained behind at his luxury apartment in New York City.

When the first photos of Deke with other women had appeared on the covers of tabloid magazines, and on entertainment channels, he'd insisted the paparazzi were just trying to make trouble for him. Rachel had believed him.

But the photos of him with other women became more frequent and more lurid, and she and Deke began spending more time apart than they did together. Rachel acknowledged her own part in the failure of the marriage; his extended absences had bothered her less and less. She wanted more in her life than an absentee husband, and a constant stream of parties with people she neither knew nor especially liked.

Finally, Rachel had moved out of his apartment. She'd determinedly found another job in the personal concierge business, even though it had meant starting at the bottom again. But when Deke didn't answer her calls or respond to her messages, she couldn't bring herself to tell him the marriage was over via a text message, so she'd flown to his oceanfront villa in California, where she knew he was staying.

The Los Angeles mansion had been filled with people—supermodels and socialites and various celebrities—and Deke had seemed surprised but unenthusiastic to see Rachel. She'd asked to speak to him privately, but he'd insisted whatever she needed to say could be said in front of his friends. When she told him she wanted a divorce, he'd gone quiet. At first, Rachel had thought he seemed surprised, but then realized he was angry and embarrassed.

He'd accused her of overreacting, claiming the marriage had failed because of her. He'd said some other things, too. Hurtful things, meant to embarrass and humiliate her in front of his assembled friends. Things she couldn't help but wonder were true. Two years had passed since she'd seen Deke, but the memories of that day were still raw.

She was so done with younger, good-looking men.

Which was why she wasn't going to so much as look at a guy like Jamie Colter in that way ever again. If she did decide to get married again—and that was a huge *if*—she'd look for an older, settled man who would appreciate her and all she had to offer. She wouldn't go near a guy like Jamie Colter, no matter how drop-dead sexy he might be.

Pushing away the disturbing memory of Jamie's broad shoulders, honed chest and small, flat nipples, she turned her attention to unpacking the suitcase that lay open on her bed. Scattered on the bedspread were her toiletries and other essentials she had grabbed before fleeing New York City and everything it represented. Eventually, she'd have to go back. She still needed to move her belongings out of her apartment. The small studio in Brooklyn was a far cry from the luxurious penthouse in Manhattan, where she and Deke had lived together during the early months of their married life, but it had suited Rachel just fine.

"Hey, kiddo…are you doing okay?"

Rachel raised her head to see her mother, Diane, standing in the doorway. Rachel shrugged and gave a wan smile. "As well as can be expected. Thanks for letting me move back in until I figure out what I'm going to do."

"This is your home, and you're welcome to stay for as long as you want. I hope you don't mind staying in the guest room. Your grandparents can't do the stairs when they come to visit, and I turned your old bedroom into a sewing room years ago."

"Honestly, Mom, I don't mind where I sleep. You could put me in a tent in the backyard, and I'd be happy."

Her mother came into the room and sat on the edge of the bed. "Do you want to go back to New York?"

"No!" Rachel exclaimed, and realized it was true. She'd lived on the East Coast since she'd graduated college, twelve years earlier. After graduation, she'd worked as a hotel concierge in New York City, before branching out as a personal concierge, working for a global company, which was how she'd met Deke.

"There's nothing left for me back there, and it's time I moved on. I thought I'd take some time off, and then maybe open an office in the Monterey or Santa Barbara area, since the business is exploding right now. There must be some celebrities who need a personal concierge. Or maybe I'll just cater to busy moms; they're at least grateful for the extra help."

"What about your job in New York?"

"I'm quitting." Rachel grimaced and sat down next to her mother. "I don't want to risk running into Deke, or any of his friends. I think it's better if I just leave, and start over. Again."

"Oh, honey." Her mother wrapped her in a comforting hug. "It just goes to show money can't buy you love. You deserve so much better than Deke Narducci, even with his millions."

Silently, Rachel agreed. Deke's trust fund had ensured a lavish lifestyle filled with luxury homes and expensive cars, but she doubted he had ever truly loved her. She pulled away from her mother's embrace. "Well, it's over now. Once I sell the car, I'll be able to pay you some rent."

Her mother's face registered surprise. "Didn't you get a divorce settlement?"

Rachel looked away, embarrassed. "Deke had an ironclad prenup, Mom, that basically denied me anything if we divorced before we had kids. I loved him, so I didn't care. I never thought the marriage would end like it did. He gave me the car just before we separated, so it's legally mine and worth quite a bit of money. He can keep the rest; I have no interest in his stupid trust fund, or anything else that belongs to him."

"Of course not. You'll be fine." Her mother smiled brightly. "In fact, I've already found a client for you."

"Oh?" Rachel braced herself. Her mother performed volunteer work at a nearby senior center, and Rachel wouldn't put it past her to try and drum up some business with the elderly residents.

"Do you remember Sharon Colter's son, Jamie?"

Rachel stared at her mother in disbelief. "No, Mom—"

Her mother raised a hand to forestall Rachel's protest. "Just hear me out. He's in the Marines, and he's home recovering from a badly broken leg and some other injuries. We booked our cruise with the Colters months ago, long before Jamie was injured. I know Sharon is beside herself at the thought of leaving him alone for two weeks, since he's unable to drive or get around, and I think it would be a perfect solution if you could look out for him while we're gone. You could bring him to his doctor appointments, pick up some groceries and beer for him, that sort of thing."

"Mom," Rachel groaned, "I'm not sure that's such a good idea."

Her mother looked bemused. "Why not? It's only for two weeks. Sharon is willing to pay you for your time, and I know Jamie would appreciate the help." She smiled fondly. "He's such a sweet boy."

Images of Jamie, bare-chested and supremely muscled, flashed through Rachel's mind. *Sweet boy* was hardly how she would describe him. Sexy beast, maybe. Hot stud, definitely. The guy was freaking gorgeous, and his smile did things to her equilibrium that scared the hell out of her. His voice alone caused shivers to chase their way along her spine. There was no way she wanted to be at his beck and call for the next two weeks, especially if he was in the habit of walking around in nothing but a pair of workout shorts.

"Where is Dylan when you need him?" she muttered. If her brother were home, she could argue he should keep an eye on Jamie, since the two had been best friends since forever.

"Dylan has a full-time job," her mother said. "He's battling a wildfire in Idaho, and they say it could be weeks before they have it contained. Besides, this is what you do. You're good at it."

"I don't think so, Mom. I hope you haven't already told

Mrs. Colter I'll do it."

"Of course I did." Her mother sounded indignant. Then, seeing Rachel's mutinous expression, she softened her tone. "You can't refuse, darling. Sharon's my best friend, and after everything she's been through, she really needs this vacation. Do it for me. Please."

Rachel sighed, her resistance slipping. "Fine," she finally muttered. She stood up. "But I am not playing nursemaid to the guy. I'll drive him to his appointments and I'll run basic errands for him, but that's it." She gave her mother a warning look. "And my hours are strictly nine to five. He's on his own outside of that time."

Her mother gave her a falsely sweet smile. "But your website states you're available twenty-four hours per day, seven days per week."

Rachel gave her mother a tolerant look. "That was when I worked as part of a concierge company. They have a staff of four hundred assistants, all over the world. Now it's just me. Besides, I can't imagine any kind of scenario where Jamie Colter would require my services after five p.m."

"Can't you?"

Rachel gave her mother a sharp look, but the older woman's face was blandly innocent.

"No," she said clearly. "I can't."

"Well, what if it's an emergency? For instance, if he falls down and can't get up," her mother clarified.

"Then what he needs is a medical alert and not a personal concierge," Rachel suggested.

Her mother just looked at her, silent.

"Fine." Rachel threw up her hands. "I'll be there if it's an emergency."

"Thank you, darling." Beaming at her success, her mother gave her a swift hug. "I knew you wouldn't let me down. I'll go tell Sharon; I know she'll be so relieved!"

Rachel listened to her mother's footsteps retreat down the hallway, followed by the slam of the front door. Crossing to the window, she watched as her mother walked the short distance to the Colter house, and rang their doorbell. After a moment, the door opened, and Rachel strained to get a better look. Jamie answered, still wearing the shorts, but now he also wore a bright red T-shirt. She watched as he moved back and invited her mother into the house. Was it just her imagination, or did he glance directly at her window before he closed the door again? Rachel stepped quickly away, not wanting him to see her.

The thought of being Jamie's personal concierge for the next two weeks unnerved her, which was ridiculous. She'd managed the personal affairs of countless clients, from millionaires to single moms, and everyone in between. Except for Deke, she'd never had a problem keeping the relationship strictly professional, and she'd never had any issues with her clients overstepping those professional boundaries.

So why did she have this nervous, fluttering sensation in

the pit of her stomach at the very thought of doing anything personal for Jamie?

"IS THAT EVEN a real thing?"

Jamie's father, Alex, looked up from his newspaper to where Jamie leaned against the kitchen counter, a cold beer in one hand.

"Is what a real thing?"

"A personal concierge." Jamie made air quotes with his free hand. "I'm pretty sure you're all just making this up so I'll feel better about having a babysitter while you're on your cruise."

His father grinned. "Are you complaining?"

"No, I'm not complaining. I'm just curious as to what a personal concierge actually does."

His father gave a snort of laughter and returned his attention to his paper. "Not what you're thinking, I promise you."

Jamie's mother chose that moment to walk into the kitchen. Giving her son an amused look, she began setting the table for dinner. "A personal concierge is absolutely a real thing. Rachel even has a website that outlines her standard services and rates."

Behind her back, Jamie exchanged a knowing look with his father. "And just what do those services include?" He had to bite the inside of his cheek to keep from grinning. His mother wouldn't appreciate his lewd humor.

Setting the dinner plates on the table, she straightened and looked at him, one hand on her hip. "Think of her as your temporary mother while I'm gone. Anything I would do for you, she'll do for you."

Jamie pulled a face. "There you go, Mom, ruining my fantasy. I absolutely cannot think of Rachel McCafferty as my substitute mother." He gave an exaggerated shudder. "Not even close."

His mother laughed and patted his cheek, before reaching behind him for some glasses. "Then think of her as your sister. And it's Rachel Narducci, not McCafferty."

Jamie took a long swallow of his beer. No way could he think of Rachel as his sister, not when his imagination was actively conjuring up all kinds of lecherous images of them together.

"She's divorced, Mom," he finally said, forcing his thoughts in a safer direction. "She probably prefers McCafferty, considering her ex is such a dick."

"Jamie!" his mother exclaimed in a reproving tone. "Why would you say such a thing? You only met the man once, and that was years ago."

"I know his type. He's an entitled, rich kid who's never worked a day in his life, and expects everyone to bend over backward whenever he walks into a room." He gave a snort of disgust. "She's better off without him."

"Well, I know he was somewhat younger than Rachel, so maybe he just wasn't ready to settle down," his mother mused. "Everyone knows boys don't mature as quickly as girls."

"I'm younger than Rachel," Jamie said, feeling suddenly defensive. "Do you think I'm immature?"

His mother looked at him, astonished. "Of course not, but it's hardly the same. You were always ahead of your years, even as a child. And being in the military does something to a person. Makes them grow up faster."

"Would you say I'm ready to settle down?" he persisted.

His mother gave him a bemused look. "Where is this coming from? Is there someone in your life you haven't told us about? A girlfriend in Oceanside?"

"No. I'm just curious what you think."

"Okay." His mother considered him for a moment. "I think one day you'll make a wonderful husband and father, but right now you're too young."

"I'm twenty-six," he countered. "There are plenty of guys in my unit who are married and have kids, and some are even younger than me."

"Jamie," said his father, sending him a wink from over the top of his paper. "This isn't a conversation you're going to win. Suffice to say a mother never thinks her son is old enough to be married, and no woman is ever going to be good enough for her boy."

"All I'm saying is there's no rush. You're young, and you

still have plenty of time before you need to think about settling down." His mother gave him a bright smile. "Besides, you haven't even met anyone, yet!"

She was wrong. Maybe his interest in Rachel McCafferty was nothing more than the remnants of a childhood crush, but he doubted it. His response to seeing her again after so many years had been completely adult in nature and, unless he had misread her, she'd had a similar reaction. Now he needed to find out if there was more to it than just physical attraction.

He had two weeks.

Chapter Three

RACHEL SAT AT the kitchen island, sipping her coffee and staring moodily at the digital clock over the oven. It was just nine a.m. She'd been up since dawn, partly because her body was still on East Coast time, and partly because her parents and the Colters had left for the airport around five a.m., and she'd risen to say good-bye to them.

But that had been hours ago, and she'd already showered, dressed, and consumed more than her daily share of caffeine. Now she wondered how she would fill the remainder of the day. She hadn't been back to Glacier Creek in a couple of years, so she could head into town and do some shopping, or maybe just sit by the lake. Neither option appealed to her.

Should she go across the street to check on Jamie, or wait for him to contact her? They hadn't even seen each other since that first morning in the driveway, never mind talked about what he might need from her in the way of personal concierge services.

Did he even know she'd been hired to provide those services to him? Her mother had assured her he'd been told, and that he was delighted. But what if she'd fibbed? Jamie wasn't like her usual clients, who were either too rich or too lazy to do anything for themselves. He might actually resent her interference in his life. Not everyone appreciated a helping hand. Aside from running a few routine errands, she couldn't foresee him asking much of her.

Setting her coffee mug down, she stood up and grabbed her tablet. Better to just get it over with. With luck, he might decide he didn't need any help from her while his parents were gone, and she could just focus on getting her own life in order. She strode across the street before she could change her mind, and rang the doorbell. Several long minutes passed while Rachel stood on the steps clutching her tablet with hands that were damp with nerves, her heart beating hard. When there was no answer, she turned away, feeling a rush of both relief and disappointment.

The door opened.

She turned back, an apologetic smile pasted on her face, and her mouth fell open. Jamie stood in the doorway, looking overtly male and extremely aggravated. She didn't have to guess why. He'd obviously been in the shower. He wore nothing but a green trash bag over his injured leg, cinched tight at the thigh with duct tape, and a pair of soft, cotton shorts that clung to his damp body and revealed more of his masculine assets than they concealed. Water glistened on his naked shoulders and chest, and dripped onto the floor beneath his foot.

"Oh," Rachel finally choked, embarrassed beyond words. "I am so sorry! I had no idea you'd be in the shower!" She almost put a hand up to her eyes to prevent herself from staring at his body. His incredibly toned and muscular body. She spun away. "I'll come back later."

"No, it's fine." His voice sounded gravelly. "You're here now, and I went through all kinds of hell trying to get my shorts on when I heard the doorbell, so you might as well come in."

His words inspired a mental image of him, naked and wet and struggling to get dressed, that caused a rush of warmth to Rachel's midsection.

"I can come back," she insisted, but he'd already retreated inside, leaving her with no option but to follow him.

Despite having lived across the street her entire life, Rachel had never been inside their house, and she saw with a sense of surprise the decor was modern and fresh. A double set of French doors opened from the kitchen onto a large, backyard deck that overlooked an in-ground swimming pool. Although it was only June and still cool, two wide umbrellas had been set up near the pool chairs, and the pool itself looked clear and blue.

"How do you like your coffee?"

Jamie had pulled two mugs out of a cupboard and was pouring coffee into each.

"A little cream, no sugar."

Leaning on his crutches, he opened the fridge and withdrew a container of cream and set it on the island, before sliding her coffee toward her. Rachel couldn't help but notice the play of muscles along his ribs as he moved, and quickly occupied herself with mixing her coffee. She watched covertly as Jamie rummaged in a drawer and pulled out a pair of scissors, and then began carefully cutting away the duct tape that secured the trash bag to his thigh.

"This is the worst part," he muttered, wincing as the tape pulled at his leg hair, before finally coming free. He pushed at the plastic bag, and tried unsuccessfully to kick it away.

"Here," Rachel said quickly. "Let me."

Before he could protest, she came around the island and leaned forward to push the wet bag down the length of the plaster cast until she could work it free of his leg, taking care not to let the water touch the cast. He smelled like fresh soap and shampoo, and she could see the whorls of golden hair on his thigh above the cast, and where the tape had left a mark on his skin. Flicking her gaze upward, she saw the wide scar on his abdomen. Up close, it was shiny and pink, and disappeared beneath the elastic waistband of his shorts. Suddenly aware he wore nothing beneath the soft, damp cotton, Rachel rose jerkily to her feet. Retreating to the other side of the kitchen, she balled up the trash bag and shoved it inside the trash bin, not looking at Jamie.

"My mom told me about your personal concierge business," Jamie said, easing himself onto a stool and leaning his crutches against the counter.

"Well, it's not *my* concierge business," she said cautiously, returning to the opposite side of the island, and curling her hands around her mug of coffee. "I worked for a global organization. I was literally just one of hundreds of personal assistants."

"Worked?" he asked, arching an eyebrow. "As in past tense?"

Rachel nodded. "I'm turning in my resignation. I'm thinking about opening my own business in the Monterey or Santa Barbara area."

Jamie gave a huff of surprised laughter. "Wow. Good for you."

She peered at him. "You think it's a good idea?"

"Hell, yeah. Monterey is filled with people who have more money than motivation. You'll probably have to turn clients away."

"That's what I'm hoping," she admitted.

"Speaking of which, I understand you've offered to help me out while our folks are on vacation."

Rachel barely prevented herself from rolling her eyes, but she didn't contradict him.

"Okay," he said, grinning. "So maybe you didn't volunteer. But I appreciate you didn't refuse. If my mom had canceled the cruise and stayed home, I'm not sure what I would have done. Gone a little nuts, I think."

His expression was so forlorn that Rachel laughed. "I totally get it, and I promise not to smother you."

Jamie stopped in the act of raising his coffee cup to pin her with a meaningful look. "Oh, no," he protested. "You go right ahead and smother me as much as you'd like. You won't hear a word of protest from me."

And there it was again, a frisson of awareness that hummed in the air between them like static electricity, causing the fine hair on her arms to stand up. Rachel looked away first, unsettled by the frank challenge in his eyes. She turned on her tablet and pretended to be engrossed in pulling up her list of client services.

"Well," she began, and to her dismay her voice sounded high and breathy. She cleared her throat and strove for a more dignified tone. "I've put together a list of services you might find useful."

She slid the tablet across the counter toward him.

Jamie scanned the list and nodded. "This is just about what I had in mind. But there are a few other things I'm not sure about..."

His voice trailed off, and Rachel gave him an encouraging smile, hoping fervently he didn't take the conversation into the gutter. "Like what?"

He scrubbed a hand across the back of his neck. Rachel tried not to notice how the movement displayed his impressive bicep, or the fact his underarm hair was dark gold. She swallowed convulsively and forced herself to focus.

"Well, I do pretty well taking care of myself, but I'd rather not go a full two weeks without changing the sheets on my bed. I'm just not sure I can manage it alone." He peered at her. "Is that asking too much?"

Rachel smiled in relief. "No, of course not. I'd be happy to make your bed up each day, and change the sheets. In fact, I can do the laundry, and prepare meals for you if you'd like." She shrugged. "I'm not a gourmet chef, but I do okay."

"Jeez." He sounded impressed. "You'd do all that? I don't want to turn you into a Cinderella."

"It's only for two weeks," she said drily. "And I'm getting paid very well for doing it."

"But this must be a little different than what you're normally accustomed to doing for your clients, right?"

"I've pretty much done everything," she hedged, feeling distracted by the sight of all that exposed skin over taut muscles. "I had several single moms whom I did shopping and household errands for, so I'm not completely out of my element."

Jamie took a swallow of his coffee, seeming completely comfortable. "So what's the most bizarre request you ever had? Can you share that, or is there some confidentiality rule you can't break?"

"I do sign a nondisclosure statement for some of my clients, but in any case, I would never reveal a client's name."

Jamie leaned over the island counter. "So what's the strangest thing you ever had to do?"

The gleam of anticipation in his blue eyes was too much to resist, and Rachel found herself responding to his conspiratorial grin.

"Well," she began carefully, "I once had a client whose little girl lost her Disney pressed coin collection, so my client sent me to Orlando to visit all the pressed coin machines, and re-create her collection."

Jamie's mouth opened, and he gave a shout of laughter. "You're kidding! What are we talking about, fifty or so machines?"

Rachel gave him a tolerant look. "Try four hundred and sixty-seven machines."

Jamie whistled. "No kidding?"

"No kidding." Rachel shrugged. "From a purely cost perspective, it wasn't a hugely expensive job, but it was definitely one of the stranger things I've been asked to do."

"Have you ever had a request you couldn't deliver on?" Interpreting her warning look, he added hastily, "I mean, aside from those that are just plain illegal or immoral."

Rachel thought for a moment. "There was a client who was traveling to China for business, and he wanted a private tour of an archeological site that has never been open to the public. I did everything I could, but there was no getting around the Chinese government."

"My heart bleeds for the poor guy," Jamie said, grinning.

"We arranged for him and his wife to have a catered, moonlight dinner on top of the Great Wall, instead."

Jamie looked suitably impressed. "And here I thought you just did errands and odd jobs."

"Nope." Rachel found herself smiling back at him. "I do it all, from travel plans, and tickets to sold-out shows, to event planning, personal shopping, and holiday decorating."

They were silent for a long moment, until Rachel realized she was staring at him like a love-struck teen. Embarrassed, she dragged her attention back to her tablet, and strove for a professional, businesslike tone.

"So, um, why don't you get dressed, and I'll begin putting together some recommendations. Let's start by reviewing your daily schedule, and then we can decide what you might need."

"Sure. Give me a minute, and I'll be right back."

She watched covertly as Jamie pushed himself to his feet and positioned his crutches. He swung away from her, and she watched the play of muscles in his back as he made his way across the kitchen. Only then did she see he had a second scar on his lower back that matched the one on his abdomen. She didn't want to think about what that meant.

She tried—and failed—not to notice how fine his ass looked beneath the soft fabric of his shorts. When he finally disappeared from view, she let her head fall into her hands, and groaned.

How was she going to get through the next two weeks? How was she ever going to maintain a professional distance from the guy, when everything he did made her pulse quicken? From the teasing glint in his blue eyes, to his contagious grin and amazing body, Jamie Colter was freaking gorgeous, and she had a suspicion he was also pretty sharp. She vaguely recalled when her brother, Dylan, had left for college, Jamie had headed to the nearest Marine Corps recruitment center. Rachel's mother had been dumbfounded, and had mentioned to Rachel on more than one occasion that Jamie could have gotten an academic scholarship to any college he wanted. But he'd been intent on serving his country, instead. Call her sappy, but Rachel found that pretty appealing. Especially when compared to what her husband, Deke, had chosen to do, which was absolutely nothing aside from spending his inheritance as fast as he could.

Ex-husband, she reminded herself.

Pushing away from the counter, she walked over to the French doors and looked unseeingly at the swimming pool. How was it that just days after her divorce, she found herself looking at another man? Granted, she hadn't lived with Deke for the last two years, and she hadn't had any romantic relationships during that time. Her job had left her with little time or energy for that, and she acknowledged that marriage to Deke had done a number on her self-esteem.

But now, with this new assignment…

She had promised both her mother and Mrs. Colter she would be exclusively available for Jamie for the next two weeks. She didn't think she had imagined the interest in Jamie's eyes when he looked at her, but did she have the courage to explore just how far his interest might go?

"Hey, sorry to keep you waiting."

Rachel turned around to see Jamie making his way back into the kitchen. He'd pulled on a well-worn, faded T-shirt with the Superman logo on the front, and a more substantial pair of cargo shorts. While she missed seeing his bare chest, she silently acknowledged the soft fabric of the shirt did nothing to detract from the hard planes of his chest.

"No worries," she replied, keeping her tone light. Coming to stand beside him, she opened her tablet with a swipe of her finger across the screen, and pulled up the standard questionnaire she used for all her clients. "Let's start with a few basic questions. What time do you typically get up in the morning?"

"Depends on what time I go to bed the night before," he said, slanting her a lazy grin. "And what I'm doing after I go to bed. I don't always sleep."

His suggestive words immediately conjured up erotic images that sent heat flooding into Rachel's face, even as her heartbeat accelerated. It had been years since a guy had made her feel the way Jamie made her feel now—sexy and desirable. But the thought of being with Jamie—of being with someone so virile and gorgeous and *young*—brought back all the insecurities she'd tried so hard to get past after her marriage to Deke had disintegrated. Because if what Deke had said was true, she was too boring and uptight to appeal to any man. Did she have the courage to prove him wrong?

Chapter Four

STANDING NEXT TO Rachel, breathing in her scent and feeling the warmth she radiated, was sheer hell. Jamie's hands curled around the handles of his crutches, when all they really wanted to do was bury themselves in the thick, silky waves of her hair.

He was pushing the boundaries of their business arrangement, but he couldn't seem to help himself. He had her to himself for the next two weeks, and he was damned well going to use every second to his own advantage. If that made her uncomfortable, then too bad. He was uncomfortable, too, and the way he saw things, there was only one way to cure that.

He intended to take Rachel to bed.

As soon as possible.

But in order to do that, he couldn't pussyfoot around the issue. She needed to know he wanted her. He sensed that she wasn't the kind of woman who slept around, or fell easily into bed with anyone. Normally, he'd respect that and not assert himself, but time was working against him. He'd been given this one chance, and he wasn't going to blow it.

Now she avoided eye contact and focused on the tablet that lay on the counter. But her breathing quickened and pink color seeped slowly into her face. She was aware of him.

Big time.

"Assuming you don't stay up all night," she continued, "what time are you normally up and dressed? I came over at nine o'clock, and you were in the shower. So is it safe to say you're ready and dressed by nine-thirty?"

He didn't miss the slight emphasis on the word *dressed* and he hid a smile. "Yeah, that's probably about right."

"Okay, so why don't I come over at ten each morning? We can have breakfast together, and then decide what we want to do for the day." She flicked a glance at him. "If that sounds okay to you."

Jamie barely contained his shock. He'd expected her to give him as little time as possible, and he'd been racking his brain trying to think of things that would require her to spend more time with him.

"You plan to spend the entire day with me?"

When she looked at him, surprised, he could have bitten his tongue off.

"No! I mean, I just thought—" She pressed a hand to her eyes and laughed, and gave him an apologetic smile. "Of course not. That would be presumptuous. What I *meant* to say is we can decide over breakfast if you'll require my services that day, or not. Does that sound acceptable?"

"Sure." Jamie nodded. "That sounds great, but let's make

it nine-thirty. I don't think either of us wants to wait until ten o'clock to eat."

He watched as Rachel bent over the tablet and tapped in the information. "Okay, so that's done. What about groceries? I'm sure your mom stocked everything before she left, but you'll need some fresh produce and dairy products at some point. Where do you prefer to shop?"

"I don't."

Rachel looked at him, and raised her eyebrows. "You don't shop?"

"I don't have a preference. Wherever you want to go is fine by me."

"Ralph's it is, then," she said. "I'll take an inventory of your cupboards, and pick up whatever else you need on Tuesday." She glanced at him. "What about doctor appointments?"

"I have an appointment with an orthopedic surgeon next week," he confirmed. "It's at the VA hospital in Kalispell, to finally get the cast taken off."

"Okay, that's good. Let me know the specifics so I can put it in my calendar." She gave him a swift appraisal. "You look fit, aside from your leg. We should probably get you out of the house each day. Go to the park, or maybe take a drive somewhere. Have you done that yet?"

Jamie shrugged. "Once, but it was fairly uncomfortable. I can't see myself fitting into your Porsche."

"That's not a problem," she assured him. "I'll rent a van

or an SUV, and remove the middle seat. You can sit in the back with plenty of room for your leg."

Jamie stared at her. "Isn't that a little extravagant?"

She leaned against the counter and looked at him in puzzlement. "Why is that extravagant? Don't you deserve to live as normal a life as possible during your recovery? Why should you stay cooped up here, when you could get out and do things? I mean, unless you're in pain, then I'd understand."

Jamie shook his head. "No, I'm not in pain."

Not much, anyway. And not enough to make him turn down the offer she was extending. Even the cost of the rental vehicle was worth it. He'd been saving his money for the past few years in order to build a little place somewhere nearby. A couple hundred bucks for a rental wasn't going to break him financially. He knew Rachel hadn't given the added expense a second thought. She was probably accustomed to clients who were rolling in money and willing to pay top dollar for the smallest convenience. He might not be rich, but he'd pay whatever price she asked if it meant spending more time in her company.

"Good, then it's settled." She smiled brightly. "I'll head up to Whitefish and pick up a vehicle this morning, so start thinking about where you might like to go. That reminds me—" She broke off and gave him a doubtful look. "Do you have a wheelchair?"

"I do."

"Great, because if you think you're just going to sit in the car while I chauffeur you around, think again. We are getting out and moving." Before he could respond, she turned back to her tablet. "So that takes care of the main issues. We'll figure the rest out as we go along."

Jamie felt a little dazed. He'd been so certain Rachel would try to find reasons not to spend time with him, yet here she was, inserting herself neatly into his life as if it was the most natural thing in the world. He had to remind himself that for her, this was just a job. She'd likely do the same thing for any other poor bastard. The thought deflated his ego just a bit.

"Sounds good," he responded, and hitched his crutches beneath his arms. "Is that it?"

If she noticed his surly tone, she gave no indication. She consulted her tablet and nodded in satisfaction. "I think so. I just need your cell phone number. I can't help you if I can't reach you."

Jamie watched as she punched his number into her phone, and then gathered up her tablet. Up close, her skin was fine and creamy, and he could see a tiny pulse beating at the base of her slender throat. She wore a deep pink, sleeveless blouse with a pair of jeans, and her arms were slim and toned. The denim hugged the curve of her hips like a second skin. Jamie ached to touch her.

"So we're done?"

"For now. I'll go get a car for us. I should be back after

lunch, so think about what you might like to do this afternoon." She glanced outside. "It looks like it's going to be a beautiful day."

"Why are you doing this?"

Rachel turned back to him, her eyes wide. "Doing what?"

He gave her a patient look. "You don't need to cater to me. I'm perfectly happy just hanging out here on my own for the next two weeks." Seeing her expression, he raised a hand. "Don't get me wrong; I'd rather spend time with you than by myself, but I don't want you to feel like you're under any obligation to do this. And don't worry—I won't rat you out to our parents. I'll tell them you took good care of me. But you don't have to sacrifice your free time for me."

"Is that what you think I'm doing?"

"Isn't it?"

She looked indignant. "I wouldn't do it if I didn't want to. As long as we're being honest, when my mother first suggested I help you out, I was against it."

"So don't do it." He could have bitten his tongue off as soon as the words left his mouth. What if she called his bluff?

"In fact," she continued, ignoring him, "right up until I came over this morning, I wasn't sure how much time I wanted to spend with you. But..."

Her sentence hung in the air between them, until Jamie took the bait.

"But what?"

She gave a shrug of one slim shoulder. "After my parents left this morning, I sat in the kitchen for nearly four hours, wondering what I was going to do for the next two weeks. Just four hours, and I was nearly crawling out of my skin with boredom."

"I'm sure you would have figured something out."

"I won't lie," she said. "I came over here thinking I'd just leave you my number and that would be it. You wouldn't want me interfering in your life, and I could at least tell my parents I offered to help you. Then we could each go our separate ways."

"So what changed your mind?"

"You did." She gave him a half smile. "If I was going stir crazy after just a few hours, how hard must it be for you—a guy accustomed to living life under the most extreme conditions—to be cooped up in a house, alone? There's only so much sun-worshipping, lounging, and sleeping that one person can do."

"I manage." His voice sounded a little rougher than he intended, because what she said was true. He was slowly going out of his mind, and the better he felt physically, the worse it became.

"Besides," she added, giving him a slow smile, "I like you."

Jamie's mood lightened. "Thanks."

"I think the next two weeks could be a lot of fun, if we keep an open mind."

Jamie looked sharply at her. Was there a hidden meaning in her words? He couldn't tell. Her face was the picture of innocence. "I think you're right," he finally agreed.

"Then it's settled. Do you want me to make some lunch for you before I leave?" she asked. "I can just put it in the fridge for whenever you're hungry."

"Nah, that's okay," he protested. "I can handle lunch. You're already doing way more than I expected."

"If you're sure…"

"Absolutely. I'll see you in a few hours. I'm just going to hang by the pool."

He stood in the doorway and watched her as she walked across the street and then maneuvered the pretty little convertible Porsche out of the garage. He lifted a hand as she drove past, wishing she didn't look so perfect in the luxury sports car.

As comfortable as he was, financially, he'd never be able to afford a car like that. He owned a motorcycle and a beat-up Land Rover that had seen better days. Both suited him just fine, but he couldn't envision Rachel driving either one. Okay, he could definitely see her sitting behind him on the motorcycle, with her legs bracketing his own, and her arms wrapped around his waist. But that sweet little fantasy would have to wait until after his cast was removed, and he went through rehab, which could be months from now.

Jamie gave a snort of disgust, and closed the front door. Here he was, envisioning a future with a woman he barely knew; a woman who had been accustomed to a much more luxurious lifestyle than what he could offer. He had no reason to think she would be willing to settle for a guy like himself. He wasn't being self-deprecating, because he wasn't a bad catch, overall, but a woman like Rachel McCafferty—he refused to think of her as Rachel Narducci—was way beyond his pay grade.

HE WAS SUFFOCATING. Darkness pressed in on all sides, and his body was wedged so tightly beneath the fallen concrete that he couldn't move.

Couldn't breathe.

He was going to die here, buried alive beneath the tons of rubble. Dust filled his nose and mouth. Someone called his name.

"Colter, help me...help me."

It was his buddy, Mike Santos, and they were trapped side by side. Jamie stretched his fingers, and touched Santos's head. Beneath his fingertips, his friend's skull crumbled, and Jamie's fingers sank into something warm and sticky.

In the darkness, someone moaned in pain.

He tried to move, and the sound came again.

Jamie realized it was him.

Something brushed his face and Jamie came awake with a start, throwing his arms up in a protective gesture, before opening his eyes. He blinked against the bright glare of sunlight, and a shadow fell across his face.

Rachel.

"Sorry," he muttered, and shoved himself higher on the chaise longue. "I must have fallen asleep."

She was bent over him and he realized the ends of her hair had brushed across his face, waking him up. Now she stretched up and adjusted the tilt of the pool umbrella until he was fully in the shade.

"You're starting to burn," she observed, standing over him.

Even under the shade of the umbrella, Jamie had to shield his eyes to look at her. The nightmare began to fade beneath the glare of the sun. "How long have you been here?"

"I just got back. Have you been asleep this whole time?"

"I guess so." He shook off the lingering grogginess and scrubbed a hand over his face. "How long have you been gone?"

"About three hours."

He *had* been asleep for the entire time she'd been gone, partly due to the meds he'd taken after she'd left. Things were getting better, though. He no longer needed to take the pills every few hours, as he had when he'd first been released from the hospital. He was down to taking just one or two doses each day, mostly for pain and partly to help him escape the memories of that shitty day in Syria, when a Russian bomber had decimated their Marine compound. But the meds were no longer keeping his nightmares at bay. Pushing the unpleasant thoughts aside, he reached for his crutches, but Rachel was there first.

"Can I help you?" she asked.

"Nope, I got it." Acutely aware of her watching him, he lifted his injured leg off the chair until he was sitting sideways, and then used his good leg and the crutches to leverage himself to a standing position. "Let's go see that rental car."

He followed her across the yard and through the gate that led to the front of the house. There, in his parents' driveway, sat a shiny white minivan.

"I thought it would be easier for you to get in and out of this, than an SUV," Rachel said, and opened the sliding door. "I had the salesman stow the middle row of seats, so there's plenty of space to move around."

Jamie stuck his head inside the van. The interior was expensive leather, with a telltale new-car smell. The dash contained all the bells and whistles of a brand-new, top-end model, and the vehicle was spotless, inside and out.

"How much did you say this is costing?" he asked cautiously.

"I didn't. It's on loan for free, for as long as we need it."

Jamie looked sharply at her. She gave him a sunny smile.

"I'm afraid to ask," he finally said.

"I decided to sell the Porsche. I brought it to a dealer in

Whitefish, and they think they can sell it." She looked almost embarrassed. "The manager fell in love with the car, so we made a deal. I get use of the van for as long as I need it, and he gets personal use of the Porsche. When I return the van, he'll sell the Porsche for me. He thinks he can get top dollar."

Jamie wanted to weep in protest. "You're selling that beauty? Why can't you just swap the cars back when we no longer need the van?"

Something flashed across Rachel's face, an expression that might have been anger, but was gone too quick for him to tell.

"I don't want it," she said firmly. "It's an impractical reminder of a life I've left behind, and Montana is no place for a Porsche."

"Well, that manager is getting the better end of the deal," he muttered. "I'd have given anything to drive that car just once."

Rachel looked unsympathetic. "What is it with you boys and your fast cars? That thing is a gas hog, and it's also dangerous. This is much more practical." She crossed her arms. "You look upset. Does this mean you no longer want to go for an outing?"

Jamie scowled. "Not when you sound like my mother. And we're not going for an *outing*. That has about as much appeal as a geriatric field trip."

Rachel laughed, and it completely transformed her. Jamie found himself transfixed by the sound of her laughter, and the way her face lit up. This was how he remembered her.

"I'm so sorry," she finally said, still smiling. "You're right; that sounded terrible. What should we call it instead?"

"Something that doesn't remotely hint at a nurse-patient or parent-child relationship," he grumbled. "What do friends call it when they go out together?"

"Are we friends?" Rachel asked, tipping her head to one side as she considered him. "I mean, I've known you for *forever*, but I wouldn't have classified you as a friend, necessarily. You were always my kid brother's sidekick. Just a baby, really."

"Never mind," Jamie said darkly. "This is just getting worse by the minute. You should stop talking now."

"We could call it a date," she offered. Seeing his surprised expression, she shrugged. "Why not? Friends go on dates, don't they?"

Not the kind of friends he had, but he wasn't about to argue with her.

"Absolutely," he agreed. "Friends do go on dates."

Thirty minutes later, with his wheelchair stowed in the rear cargo space, and his leg resting comfortably on a leather ottoman Rachel had confiscated from the living room, they were on their way.

Rachel sat in the driver's seat, and their eyes met in the rearview mirror. "Sure you're comfortable back there?"

Surprisingly, Jamie was very comfortable. The van was luxuriously appointed, and he'd had no difficulty getting into the rear seat. His only complaint was that there was too much space between them; he would have liked to be sitting in the passenger seat. He gave Rachel a thumbs-up, and sat back to enjoy the ride.

"Are you hungry?" she called.

Jamie shrugged. "Getting there. What'd you have in mind?"

She smiled at him in the mirror, and then turned in the direction of town. Within ten minutes they were pulling into the parking lot by the town pier. As Jamie eased himself into the wheelchair and settled his leg onto the extended support, he breathed in the crisp, mountain air. He hadn't seen the lake since before he'd left for Syria; hadn't realized just how much he missed being near the water.

"Man, that air smells good," he said, as she retrieved her pocketbook and locked the van.

"What shall we do first?" she asked. "We could take a stroll to the end of the pier, or go get something to eat. Red's Diner is always a good choice."

A small burger shack stood near the entrance to the pier, and the smell of fried food wafted on the air. Jamie realized he was famished. He hadn't eaten breakfast after Rachel had left that morning, and now his stomach was talking to him.

"Let's go grab some food at that little burger joint, and take it out to the pier," he suggested.

"That sounds perfect," Rachel agreed, and made to grab hold of the handles on the back of the wheelchair.

"Whoa, what are you doing?" Jamie demanded, frowning at her. "I don't need you to push me. In fact, I could use the exercise."

He demonstrated his ability by grabbing the wheels and expertly maneuvering the chair in a circle, before rocking it back into a wheelie.

Rachel raised her hands in surrender, laughing. "Okay, I get it. Sorry to violate your man-card!"

She walked beside him as they made their way across the parking lot to the pier, and he reveled in the cool breeze on his face. Two young women, dressed in shorts and soft cotton tops, who clearly weren't wearing bras, strolled past them and smiled at Jamie, before falling against each other, laughing.

He grinned broadly after they had passed. "I love when the weather turns warm."

Beside him, Rachel gave an indelicate snort. "Aren't they a little young?"

He had no interest in the girls, but he couldn't resist baiting Rachel, just a little. "I don't know," he mused. "They looked to be in their early twenties. I'm twenty-six, so I think we're in the same league. Wouldn't you agree?"

"Excuse me!" The two young women had returned, and now they were looking both sheepish and hopeful. The first girl smiled at Jamie. "We couldn't help but notice nobody has signed your cast. Would you mind if we did?"

Jamie laughed in surprise. The girls were right; the plaster was still smooth and unblemished. He spun the chair toward them.

"Be my guest," he offered.

The girls fished around in their purses until one triumphantly produced a couple of gel pens, in pink and purple. Jamie was acutely conscious of Rachel, standing just to one side, watching. He didn't look at her as the girls knelt on the wooden walkway on either side of his leg, and proceeded to draw on the cast. Their hair fell forward as they worked, obscuring their efforts.

"Thank you for letting us do this," the first girl enthused.

"Are you in the service?" The second girl glanced up at him, and her eyes swept over him, missing nothing.

Jamie nodded. "Yeah, I am."

"Oh! Did this happen in combat?"

"It did," he confirmed.

They both made little cooing sounds of sympathy, and renewed their artistic endeavors.

"There!" The first girl rose to her feet and surveyed her handiwork. "I hope you like it."

Jamie nearly groaned aloud when he saw the swirly hearts and flowers she had drawn, along with the caption, *Get Well Soon!* Beneath the hearts, her name was a looping scrawl.

"Okay, all done," declared the second girl. Standing up, she gave Jamie a shy smile. "I wrote my number, right there.

If you ever want to get out, maybe have a drink, just give me a call."

She had drawn two purple palm trees bowing toward each other, and between them, a setting sun complete with pointy rays of sunshine. In the center of the sun she'd written her name and number.

"Ah, thank you—" Jamie peered down at his leg "—Chelsea."

"You're welcome. Thank you for your service." Chelsea's smile broadened and she reached out to shake Jamie's hand. "Well, we should get going. Give us a call sometime!"

"Bye," said the first girl.

"Thanks again, ladies."

He waited until they were out of earshot before he began pushing his chair again. "They obviously don't think I'm too old for them," he observed, suppressing a grin. "And they can't be that young if they're old enough to go out for drinks."

Rachel was silent, and when he risked a glance at her, he almost regretted teasing her. He couldn't see her eyes behind her sunglasses, but he recognized the disapproving set of her jaw, and her rigid posture. He sighed inwardly. The old Rachel—the one he'd been crazy about as a teen—wouldn't have given a shit about other pretty girls, because she'd been that secure in herself. She'd had so much confidence, and such a zest for life that she hadn't concerned herself with petty trivialities like jealousy or self-doubt.

While she seemed efficient and confident in her abilities as a personal concierge, Jamie sensed a change in her. She seemed more tightly wound than he remembered, and there was less laughter in her than before. Jamie wanted to reassure her the girls couldn't hold a candle to her, but another part of him wanted her to recognize he was a man now, and some women actually found him attractive. In fact, he was pretty sure Rachel found him attractive, too.

Now he just had to get her to admit it.

Chapter Five

RACHEL HAD ABSOLUTELY no right to be jealous. She barely knew Jamie—had spent less than a few hours in his company. Just because they'd jokingly agreed to call their outings *dates* did not mean she had any claim on him.

But inwardly, she acknowledged she was jealous, pure and simple. Had she honestly believed a guy like Jamie would look twice at someone like her? Why would he ever be interested in a divorced thirty-three-year-old when there were dozens of young, toned, beautiful twenty-somethings all over the place?

She'd seen the way those two girls had looked at him. Not that she blamed them. He was a gorgeous guy, and with his leg in a cast, and his muscled arms displayed to full advantage as he wheeled his chair along the sidewalk, it was no wonder they had just about fallen over him. But the fact they hadn't considered her to be competition was what really stung. That second girl hadn't even glanced her way as she'd written her phone number all over Jamie's leg, and then coyly invited him out for drinks. Had they thought she was his older sister?

She shook off the unpleasant thoughts.

But Jamie's reminder that he was closer to their age than he was to hers had hit her like a solid blow. Suddenly, she felt every bit her age, and not in a good way. She told herself it didn't matter. Hadn't she resolved to find an older, safer man the next time around? Sliding a covert glance at Jamie as he cheerfully pushed his chair beside her, she felt as if she'd opted for mushy oatmeal when there was a big, juicy steak right in front of her.

As if sensing her scrutiny, he glanced at her. "What is it? Regretting your offer to spend time with me so soon?"

He sounded suspiciously cheerful.

"No, I'm not regretting my offer," she retorted. "I'm just wondering if you're going to ogle every pretty girl we pass."

They had reached the small burger shack, and got into line behind the dozen or so people waiting to place their order.

"Hey, I didn't ask them to stop and autograph my cast," he said. "But now that you mention it, what's the harm in enjoying the scenery? I spent the last year in Syria, and I haven't been anywhere in the couple of months since I've been home. Trust me when I say there's been a distinct shortage of pretty girls in my life. Why would you begrudge me this?"

Rachel crossed her arms and pretended to study the menu over the order window. "I don't begrudge you," she finally conceded, knowing she sounded grumpy.

Rachel started when a warm hand curled around her arm, drawing her attention away from the menu and toward the man by her side. When she reluctantly looked at Jamie, he had removed his sunglasses and was studying her quietly.

"You must know those girls have nothing on you," he finally said, too low for any of the nearby patrons to hear.

Furious that he found her so transparent, Rachel pulled her arm free. "I don't know what you're talking about."

To her dismay, Jamie just laughed softly. "Okay. We'll play it your way, for now." Then, louder: "But for the record, you are far and away the most beautiful woman in this town. Maybe even the most beautiful woman in Montana!"

Several people in front of them turned around, and seeing Jamie and Rachel, smiled, before exchanging knowing looks. They thought she and Jamie were a couple, which just made her feel even more pathetic.

"Jamie Colter," Rachel hissed beneath her breath, "stop, or I'll leave you here and you can find your own way home."

He was instantly contrite. "Okay. But it's the truth."

"You don't need to say that. I'm fine."

"Why can't I tell you what I think?"

Rachel gave him a warning look. Jamie put his hands up in surrender, but thankfully didn't pursue the topic.

Rachel didn't believe Jamie. He'd only said she was beautiful because she'd let him see her insecurity. She hated feeling this way: like someone had thrown a switch on a blender inside her stomach.

Deke had once confided that her confidence was what had initially drawn him to her. Hadn't someone once said people destroy those things they love most? Well, Deke had done a good job of destroying her self-confidence and making her feel unworthy.

Of him.

Of being his wife.

Of everything.

They ordered their food—a couple of cheeseburgers and a large French fry—and slowly made their way to the wide pier that extended out over the lake. The support pilings were covered in mussels, and the sound of the water as it sucked at the poles and lapped gently against the beach was a balm to Rachel's bruised ego. Sunlight danced on the water, and farther down the lake, she could see tiny white sails. Her spirits rose marginally.

Despite being early in the season, the pier was crowded with people fishing over the railing. Rachel and Jamie paused several times to watch as someone reeled in a fish. Greedy ring-billed gulls swooped low in the hopes of stealing the catch, and had to be waved away.

"They look as hungry as I feel," Jamie commented. "Let's sit over here."

He indicated one of the benches that had been built into the pier, and Rachel sat down as Jamie rolled his chair beside her, careful to keep his extended leg out of the flow of human foot traffic. He opened the paper bag on his lap and handed Rachel a burger, and then set the fries on the bench beside her.

They ate in silence for several minutes. Rachel tried and failed not to watch Jamie. He ate with gusto, making appreciative noises that caused several people to smile as they passed. For Rachel, those sounds caused her imagination to run riot. Was he that vocal during sex? She suspected he might be. The very thought caused her skin to heat in a way that had nothing to do with the afternoon sun. She took a small bite of her burger and pretended not to hear his sounds of pleasure.

"So Deke-wad really did a number on you, huh?" he finally said, taking a long swallow of water from one of the bottles she'd packed.

Rachel lowered her burger and stared at him. "How do you—what would make you say that?"

Jamie shrugged and reached for some French fries on the bench beside her. The back of his fingers brushed against her thigh, and she forced herself not to react.

"Just a hunch." He ate his fries and then leaned back in his chair, studying her from behind his sunglasses. "I don't read the tabloids because most of that shit is just that—bullshit. But I know guys like Deke Narducci, and they're threatened by anything or anyone who steals their limelight." A smile touched his mouth. "And I'm pretty sure anytime you two were in public together, you stole the show."

A wave of pleasure washed over her at the compliment. Still, she had to disagree. "If you believe that, then you obviously don't know Deke. His outfits alone stole the show."

Jamie made a scoffing sound. "He dresses like a clown. Has anyone told him how ridiculous he looks?" He made exaggerated gestures with his hands. "All that long hair and those bizarre hats he wears—" He shook his head in disgust. "Someone needs to tell him M.C. Hammer wants his pants back."

This time, Rachel did laugh. She couldn't help herself, his expression was so priceless, and there was a part of her that appreciated how he didn't gush over Deke, the way most people did.

"There it is," Jamie said, grinning. "There's that smile. That's what I remember most about you from when we were kids; your smile could just lay me out flat." He fell back in his chair with his arms flung out, as if he were dead.

Rachel laughed again. "Thank you," she finally said.

Jamie straightened. "Anytime. But I'm being sincere. That guy did not deserve you, and if he has half a brain, he's already regretting having signed those divorce papers."

Rachel pretended to be absorbed in wrapping up the remains of her lunch. "No," she finally said. "He's not regretting a thing. In fact, he's already moved on." She smiled brightly. "Several times, in fact."

"Which just proves my point. He's an idiot."

Rachel shrugged. "I'm over it. But you're right—he didn't do my self-esteem any favors." She gathered up the paper wrappings and stood to toss the trash in a nearby bin. "Ready?"

He peered up at her. "Where to now?"

"I thought we could take a walk through the downtown, but if you're getting tired, we could head home."

"Are you kidding? I feel great, and this is by far the best day I've had since I've been home."

They made their way back along the length of the pier, maneuvering slowly through the small groups of people and anglers.

"So what happened over there?" Rachel asked. "I remember seeing it on the news, and my mom told me a little bit about it, but not much."

Jamie didn't answer right away, and Rachel could sense the topic wasn't an easy one for him to talk about.

"I'm sorry," she said. "I'm not trying to pry."

"No, it's fine. Some days it seems like a lifetime ago, and other days it seems like it happened just yesterday."

They reached the end of the pier, and turned onto the sidewalk that ran the length of Main Street. Business was brisk at the burger shack, and the line extended down the pier. Families strolled along the sidewalk, window-shopping and eating ice cream. The sound of children playing in the nearby park, the sun sparkling on the water, and the sheer beauty of the day made it difficult to believe anything as ugly as war existed.

But it did. And it had exacted a terrible toll on the man sitting beside her.

“Why were you over there?” Rachel asked.

“I was part of a unit doing humanitarian work.”

Rachel accepted his explanation, even if she didn’t entirely believe it. She knew there were U.S. troops in Syria helping the Kurdish militia retake some of the cities, and Jamie’s Marine unit had likely been part of that effort.

“The strike came just before dawn, when most of our unit was asleep,” he continued. “The sirens went off, and I heard the whistle of the incoming rocket, but we didn’t even have time to grab our protective gear before the entire building just detonated.”

Rachel looked at Jamie. His jaw was set, and she could see how hard it was for him to talk about that night. She put a hand on his shoulder, and he stopped.

“I’m so sorry,” she said. “I can’t begin to imagine what you went through, but I’m so glad you’re safe, and that you’re home.”

He nodded, but didn’t look at her. “Thanks.”

Rachel drew her hand away. “You said you were trapped in the rubble.”

He drew in a deep breath and blew it out hard. “Yeah. We were on the first floor, and were pretty much buried by the two floors above us.”

“But you survived.”

"I did. I was unconscious during most of the rescue effort, but when I came to, I couldn't see anything and I thought I was going to suffocate on the dust. But I could hear them up above me, working to remove the debris." He was quiet for a moment, lost in reflection. "I could barely breathe, never mind yell to let them know I was alive. But they didn't give up, not until every member of our unit was found."

"Can I ask about your injuries? How serious were they?"

"I was busted up pretty good," he said. "The surgeon said I might always have a limp, that's how badly my leg was damaged. I think there's more metal than bone in there, now."

"And the scar on your stomach?" she asked quietly.

"That's where a piece of rebar went right through me."

Rachel gasped. She couldn't stop her horrified reaction. "You were *impaled*?"

"Pretty much," he acknowledged.

Rachel tried to imagine the scene, but the images were so horrific that she shuddered. She regretted having asked him about the incident, not because she didn't care but because she'd ruined an otherwise perfect day by bringing the subject up.

"I'm so sorry," she finally said. "I didn't mean to make you relive that again."

To her surprise, he stopped and took her hand, squeezing her fingers. "No, don't be sorry. I'm glad you asked. Being at home with my parents—they don't get it. They know, of course, but they don't talk about it. I don't know if it's because they think it's too hard for me, or because it's too hard for them."

"You're their only son," Rachel said quietly, looking down at their linked hands. "Their only child. I'm sure they're just grateful to have you safe."

"I think so. My mom drove me nuts when I was first home. She couldn't do enough for me, and was always hovering, trying to make sure I was comfortable." He gave her a lopsided smile. "They were dark days, and I wasn't a very good patient. Then one night I heard her crying when she thought I couldn't hear. That's when I finally realized how tough this whole thing has been for them, too."

"Is it better now?"

"Oh, definitely." He shaded his eyes as he looked up at her, his expression lightening. "You're here. The world is suddenly full of possibilities."

Rachel laughed. "You haven't changed a bit since you were a kid, Jamie Colter."

"Oh, Rachel," he said softly, and his voice was rich with promise. "That's where you're so very wrong."

Chapter Six

THEY FELL INTO a comfortable routine over the next several days. As promised, Rachel came over at nine-thirty each morning and they ate breakfast together by the pool, before deciding how to spend the day.

The day before, they'd driven up to Whitefish and had taken a short cruise on Whitefish Lake, before spending the afternoon browsing through the shops in the quaint downtown. At Rachel's recommendation, they'd enjoyed dinner and a couple of beers at a breezy, open-air brew pub. Jamie couldn't recall what they'd talked about, only that they had done a lot of laughing. She'd completely captivated him. She'd been all he'd remembered from their youth, and more. Several times during the evening, he'd caught her watching him when she thought he didn't notice.

It had been after ten p.m. when they'd arrived back in Glacier Creek, and they'd stood in her dark driveway for about fifteen minutes, just talking. He'd had a nearly overwhelming urge to kiss her good-night, but sensed it was still too soon. The last thing he wanted was to scare her off.

Today, however, Jamie had wanted to surprise Rachel by

cooking breakfast for her. He'd set his alarm extra early that morning, wanting to be ready for when she arrived. Now he moved around the kitchen, gathering ingredients and pans. Rachel had provided breakfast for the past two mornings, and while the meals had been tasty, Jamie found he was in the mood for something a bit more substantial than yogurt and fruit, or the homemade muffins she brought from the Gingersnap Bakery. He pulled fixings out of the fridge and cupboards and went to work, determined to surprise her.

Fifteen minutes later, he heard the front door open, and she came into the kitchen with her nose in the air, sniffing appreciatively.

"Is that bacon I smell?"

Jamie grinned as she pulled out a stool and sat down on the opposite side of the kitchen island. "Yes, ma'am."

She set a tote bag onto the floor beside her and surveyed the ingredients on the counter beside him. "Wow, this looks fabulous, Jamie, but you didn't have to go to all this trouble. I'm happy to cook breakfast."

"Absolutely not. I've been sitting around doing nothing for long enough. You, Rachel McCafferty, are in for a treat."

He had sweet potatoes and onions grilling, and now he added spicy chorizo to the mix. He was comfortable in the kitchen, and liked having Rachel there, watching him. He scooped the bacon out of the pan and set it on some paper towels to drain, and then expertly cracked four eggs into the sizzling fat.

"I'm impressed," Rachel said. "You've obviously done this before."

"Many times." Jamie indicated the toaster on the counter behind him. "Maybe you can get the toast going for me. There's a small cup of melted butter in the microwave, and a basting brush in that drawer."

Rachel did as he asked, and he was aware of her watching covertly as he scooped the potato and chorizo mixture into two shallow bowls, and then laid fresh slices of avocado on top. She buttered the bread as he laid two perfectly cooked eggs over each dish, and topped them with several slices of crisp bacon.

"That really looks fabulous, and it smells amazing," she said, putting the toast onto a separate plate. "Can I make some coffee?"

"Already done," he said cheerfully. "If you don't mind carrying everything out to the pool for me…"

Rachel looked through the connecting doors to where he'd already set the patio table, complete with a pot of coffee, and a pitcher of orange juice.

"Jamie!" she exclaimed in surprise. "That must have taken you forever! How did you get everything out there?"

"I improvised," he replied, winking at her.

Lifting the plates, Rachel went outside and set the dishes on the table. Jamie followed her, more slowly. He'd probably overdone it a bit, but he wasn't going to say anything. If Rachel thought he might be tired, she'd insist he rest and then she'd leave. No way was that happening.

"Here, let me get your chair for you," she said, studying his face. "Sure you're okay?"

"Never better."

Once they were seated, Jamie poured the coffee and juice, and began digging into his breakfast. Rachel took a forkful of the chorizo, avocado and egg, and then stared at Jamie in pleasured surprise.

"Oh, this is incredible," she declared. "I can't recall the last time I had something so delicious."

"It's the spices," Jamie offered, taking a swallow of coffee. "But don't ask, because it's a secret family recipe."

Rachel laughed softly. "Oh, okay. Well, I'm asking your mother for the recipe when she gets home, and don't try to stop me."

Jamie grinned. "Good luck with that. Like I said, it's a family secret, so you'll have to marry me if you want it."

Rachel pretended dismay. "Is that a proposal?"

Jamie looked sharply at her, his fork halfway to his mouth. "Would you accept?"

For a moment, he saw something in her eyes that made him believe she was going to say yes. Then she took a hasty sip of her coffee, avoiding his eyes. "I'm too old for you."

Jamie barely suppressed a scoffing sound of disgust. "What are you, thirty-two?"

"I just turned thirty-three."

"So? Big deal." He let his gaze travel slowly over her.

"Look at you—you're in better shape than most women in their twenties."

Rachel slid him a tolerant look. "Thanks."

Jamie shrugged and forced himself to continue eating. The topic intrigued him, since he suspected Rachel had a huge chip on her shoulder about her age. In his opinion, thirty-three was still young. He wanted to convince her their age difference didn't matter to him, but he didn't think she'd appreciate hearing that.

"You act as if you're over the hill," he said. "Haven't you heard thirty is the new twenty?"

"That makes you about thirteen, then," she retorted, but she smiled as she said it, taking the sting out of the words.

"Hey, how's Dylan doing these days?" he asked, thinking it might be wise to change the subject.

"He's doing fine, from what I understand," she replied. "I haven't seen him recently, but he's been battling a wildfire in Idaho for a couple of weeks now."

"I'm hoping I have a chance to see him before I return to duty."

Rachel gaped at him. "You're actually going back?"

Jamie lowered his fork. "Of course. It's my job."

"But why can't you find another job?" she persisted. "Maybe one where crazy people aren't dropping bombs on your head?"

Jamie carefully wiped his mouth. "I've wanted to be a Marine since I was a kid." How could he explain it to her so she would understand? "Those guys and gals in my unit are my family. I can't just turn and walk away, Rachel."

He could see the distress in her dark eyes. "But what about your leg? Will they even let you come back?"

"Hmm. That could be a problem," he admitted.

His leg had been crushed. He'd had four different surgeries on the leg alone. He'd lain in a Bethesda hospital bed for nearly a month with an external fixator on his leg. More than a dozen screws had been attached to his broken bones through small incisions in the skin and muscle, attached to a metal frame on the outside of his leg. The contraption had looked like a mad scientist's bad experiment. Once the bones had stabilized, they'd removed the external frame, and had put the leg in a cast. He still had plates and screws attached to the bones themselves. He hoped to regain enough strength in the limb to resume his duties, but nothing was certain.

"Couldn't you ask for a job where you don't have to deploy?" Rachel asked.

"Like a desk job?" He couldn't keep the derision out of his voice. "I'd rather be dead than be cooped up in some office every day."

Rachel's expression grew shuttered, and she abruptly pushed her chair back. "I'm not hungry anymore. Why don't I clear the dishes?"

"Rachel—"

Damn. He'd upset her.

She picked up her plate and made to move past him, but

he caught her wrist and drew her to a stop. She didn't look at him, but neither did she protest when he took the plate from her and set it back on the table, and then drew her down onto his good leg.

"Jamie," she protested softly. "Your leg..."

"Shh. It's fine," he assured her. "I want you to stop worrying about me, okay?"

She bowed her head. She was so close, her breath was a soft puff of warmth against his cheek. He slid a hand beneath the heavy fall of dark hair and lightly cupped her face, letting his fingers trace the delicate contours of her jaw, her ear, her neck. Her breath caught, and it took no more than a slight tilt of his head to press his mouth gently against hers.

She stilled, and her body went rigid. Then she gave a soft exhalation, and her lips moved tentatively against his, returning his kiss. She tasted like sweet orange juice. She leaned in to him, and one hand crept to his shoulder, and then curled around his neck. Jamie made a sound of approval and angled his head for better access.

Her lips were soft and lush, and he could have luxuriated in their moist plumpness all morning, but the last thing he wanted was to scare Rachel off. However reluctantly, he would release her. But before he could break the kiss, she opened her mouth and touched her tongue to his lips.

Jamie was lost.

With a soft groan of surrender, he fused his mouth to hers, reveling in the hot slickness of her tongue as she pressed forward. She made a humming sound of pleasure that went straight to his groin and caused his body to react. Jamie had gone without sex—or intimacy of any kind—for more than a year. Now the impact of those long months of forced celibacy hit him with all the force of a sledgehammer, more so because it was Rachel in his arms, kissing him as if her life depended on it.

She slid her arms around his neck, deepening the kiss. Jamie buried his hand in the silken mass of her hair and explored her more fully, tasting her. She shifted on his lap, and in another second she would realize just how badly he wanted her. Reluctantly, he pulled away.

Rachel's breathing was swift and uneven, and for a long moment they just stared at each other. Then she stood up, retrieved the dishes from the table, and fled indoors. Jamie blew out his breath and sagged back in his wheelchair.

Goddamn.

He cursed the busted leg that prevented him from following her inside and carrying her into his bedroom.

He sat on the patio for several long minutes to regain control of his rampant lust. Just as he made the decision to grab his crutches and go after her, Rachel appeared in the doorway. She came over to the table and sat down across from him.

"I'm sorry," she finally said. She gestured helplessly. "I didn't mean for that to happen, and I won't blame you if you want to fire me."

Jamie gaped at her. "*Fire you*? Are you kidding me?"

Rachel gave a self-conscious shrug. "I crossed the line."

Jamie sat back in his chair and considered her. "It was a kiss, Rachel. One that I initiated. And I'll be damned if I'll feel bad about it."

Rachel drew in a breath. "Thanks. I just don't want you to think I'm some sort of Mrs. Robinson, who takes advantage of younger men."

"You're not?"

"Of course not!"

"That's a damn shame," Jamie said, with heartfelt regret.

When Rachel laughed, he relaxed a bit. For a moment, he'd been certain she would quit. He didn't want to pressure her, but their time together was limited. He just needed to convince her how good they could be together, although he knew she'd felt the chemistry. Rachel had definitely been into that kiss. He'd been the one to pull away first, and he hadn't misread her reaction to him.

She wanted him.

He knew the difference in their age bothered her, but as far as he was concerned, it was a non-issue. Rachel might still think of him as a kid, but he'd had his shit together for a long time, and he knew what he wanted in life. He had a sweet little condo that overlooked the ocean in California, with plans to build a timber-frame house here in Glacier Creek, both for when he had some vacation time, and for when he eventually left the military. He was financially secure, and he had no problems with commitment. In fact, he considered himself a pretty good catch. So what if he didn't have the money or fame Deke Narducci had? Look how that had turned out for Rachel.

He watched as her face bloomed with color over his remarks. Man, he loved to watch her squirm. Now she looked at him, and he could see her struggling to compose herself.

"I have something planned for today that I think you'll enjoy," she finally said, changing the subject.

"Rachel, you don't have to do that." Didn't she know just spending time with her was enough?

"Do what?"

"You don't have to entertain me," he said patiently. "I'm perfectly happy just hanging out. In fact, you could go grab your swimsuit and we could just spend the day here, by the pool. I can grill us something for lunch, and we can just have a laid-back day."

She wavered for a moment, and Jamie knew she was tempted.

"C'mon," he urged. "You've been great, shuttling me all over the place for the past few days. Don't get me wrong; it's been fun, but maybe a down day is just what we need."

Rachel immediately looked alarmed. "Have I been pushing you too hard? I didn't even ask if these were things you wanted to do."

Jamie laughed, and shook his head. "No, you haven't been pushing me. But why don't we just stay here today?

The temps are supposed to get up near eighty today, so it would be nice for you to be able to take a swim."

"Oh!" she exclaimed, pushing her chair back and standing up. "That reminds me—I have something for you!"

He watched with interest as she retrieved her tote bag from the kitchen and carried it out to the patio. Reaching inside, she drew out a box and put it on the table in front of him.

"It's a waterproof protector for your cast," she said, smiling. "This way, you won't have to use a trash bag with duct tape."

She leaned over his shoulder as he read the instructions on the back, and Jamie reacted instantly. She smelled incredible. Her hair fell forward and brushed against the side of his face and neck. He needed only to turn his head to press his mouth against her cheek. Frowning, he forced himself to focus on the box.

"See?" she said, pointing to a picture diagram. "This bag will fit over your cast and form an airtight vacuum seal to keep water out. And there's no tape involved, so it won't be like ripping off a Band-Aid every time you use it."

"Can I swim with it?" he asked.

Opening the box, he pulled out the blue, rubbery cover and examined it, while Rachel reviewed the instructions.

"This says you can swim with it," she said doubtfully. "But I'm not sure I'd want to take the chance."

He tipped his head back and grinned up at her. "Then

why did you buy it? It's either going to work, or it's not, whether I'm in the shower or the pool."

Rachel stood up, gathering the rest of the breakfast dishes from the table. "Okay. I'll just bring these into the house and go change into a swimsuit, and then I'll be right back."

"Take your time," Jamie said as she retreated indoors. "I'm not going anywhere."

Chapter Seven

RACHEL RETURNED THIRTY minutes later to find Jamie had changed into a pair of swim trunks, patterned in varying shades of blue that reminded her of rippling water. He had removed his shirt, and was relaxing under the umbrella in one of the chaises. For a moment, Rachel just stood in the doorway to the patio and stared at him.

He had been shirtless that first day she'd returned home, when she'd found herself literally speechless at the sight of him. Even relaxed as he was now, the sheer physicality of him was impressive. He had one arm bent beneath his head, and Rachel swallowed hard at the sight of his bicep. Despite the long weeks he'd spent in a hospital, his skin was a warm, golden color and the muscles in his chest and abs were more than evident. She didn't doubt even with his injury, he'd found a way to work out and stay in shape. She crossed the patio to the empty chaise and set her tote bag on the ground between their chairs.

Jamie cracked one eye open and peered at her, and that sliver of bright blue was enough to cause Rachel to blush all over.

"You have too many clothes on," he observed. His voice was gravelly with sleep.

Rachel kicked off her sandals and perched on the edge of the recliner, but chose to keep her white linen cover-up on. Although it was lightweight and sheer, it came down to her knees and had long, billowy sleeves. There was no need to keep wearing it, since she was in the shade, but no way was she going to remove her only protection from Jamie's sharp gaze.

She'd spent too much time debating over whether to wear the one-piece Speedo, or the bikini. She'd finally decided the Speedo might make her seem less confident about her body, so had reluctantly opted for the bikini. She kept herself in good shape, but the small signs of her age were there, for those who cared to look closely. And she had a suspicion Jamie missed nothing.

He pushed himself higher on his chaise, and adjusted the backrest so he was no longer reclining. Reaching down, he retrieved the latex cast protector from where it lay on the ground between them, and held it out to Rachel.

"Okay, let's check this thing out," he said. "I can usually get a trash bag over my foot, because it's loose, but I think I'm going to need your help getting this on."

Rachel took the protector from his hands, and told herself it did not resemble an enormous, blue condom. Only, it sort of did. Standing up, she moved to the foot of his chaise and looked doubtfully at his leg.

"Are you sure?"

"Definitely." He raised his leg off the recliner and waggled his toes at her. "See? No worries."

"Okay." Taking the protector in her hands, she worked it over the bottom portion over his foot. Jamie tried to help by holding his leg up and away from the chair. Rachel pulled the latex over his knee, and then realized she was quickly running out of cast. Any further, and her fingers would encounter the warm, golden skin of his thigh.

"Can you take it from here?" she asked, trying to sound casual.

Jamie wasn't fooled. "Coward," he accused softly, but took hold of the rubber edge and deftly pulled it up to his thigh.

Using the attached squeeze bulb, Rachel sucked the excess air out of the protector until Jamie's leg was literally vacuum sealed inside the latex.

"Nice," he said, smoothing his fingers over his leg. "There's no way any water is getting inside." He looked up at Rachel and smiled, and her insides went a little mushy. "Thank you."

"Of course."

She stepped back as Jamie swiveled his leg to the side of the chaise, and reached for his crutches. Rachel handed them over, and watched as he deftly rose to his feet. He looked over the pool.

"Should I use the steps, or the diving board?"

"Jamie!"

She was honestly shocked he would even consider jumping off the diving board with his injured leg.

"The steps," he confirmed, seeing her expression. Sliding his sunglasses over his eyes, he adjusted his crutches under his arm.

"Here, let me help you."

"Nope, I got this."

Rachel watched as he made his way to the shallow end of the pool, sat down at the top of the wide steps that led into the water, and laid his crutches aside. Still seated, he lowered himself into the water, one step at a time, until he was floating up to his chest.

"Ah," he breathed, rotating his arms in the water. "This feels incredible." He looked up at her and grinned. "C'mon in, the water's great!"

The cool blue of the water did look inviting. Rachel couldn't recall the last time she'd just enjoyed being in the sun and water. There was no way she could shed her cover-up and get into the pool without Jamie seeing her, so she just took a deep breath and pulled the gauzy garment over her head, and tossed it onto the nearby chair.

"You look...incredible," Jamie said. "That's, er, a good color on you."

The raspberry bikini probably made her skin seem even whiter, if that was possible, and Rachel resisted the urge to look down at herself, just to be sure everything was adequately covered. Then, aware of Jamie's eyes on her, she walked to the steps and made her way into the water with as much grace as she could manage.

"There," Jamie said, when she was finally floating beside him. "Doesn't that feel good?"

"It does," she agreed. "How is your leg?"

"Never better," he assured her. "Nice and dry."

He had sidled up beside her, and before she could react, he put a hand on top of her head and pushed her beneath the surface. She came up, spluttering and indignant, slicking her wet hair back from her face.

"Why did you do that?" she demanded, when she could speak.

Jamie laughed, unrepentant. "Because you looked so uptight and self-conscious. Be glad I have a broken leg, otherwise I would have picked you up and thrown you into the deep end."

"Why, you—" Mindful of his leg, Rachel braced her hands on his shoulders and attempted to return the favor. But instead of going under, Jamie hauled her against his chest.

Rachel could have pushed away. It would have been easy enough to do. Instead, she let him steer them into deeper water. She wasn't going to fool herself into believing she hadn't seen this coming, or that it wasn't exactly what she'd hoped might happen. Jamie was a gorgeous man, and she *would* be kidding herself if she said she didn't find everything about him sexy as hell.

She slid her arms around his neck, and he held her in place with one strong hand against her back. His body was warm and sleek and muscular, and the water sloshing between them made wet, sucking noises. Knowing she was heading into dangerous—forbidden—territory, Rachel slid her leg against his good one, reveling in the slippery-rough sensation against her sensitive skin.

He propelled them to the side of the pool and kept them balanced there with one arm on the edge, before removing his sunglasses and setting them on the tiles.

"What are you doing?" Rachel asked.

"What I've been wanting to do since I first saw you getting out of that Porsche," he muttered, and lowered his head.

The kiss was hot.

Searing.

Rachel had expected the sweet tenderness of their earlier kiss, but this one obliterated that memory. This was something primal, urgent. Jamie's mouth slanted over hers, and his tongue mated with hers in a slick, hot glide that made her muscles clench, and her bones go soft. She shifted closer, and there was the unmistakable thrust of his arousal against her abdomen. The sensation caused an instant reaction, as her sex bloomed with heat.

She became aware her hands were stroking Jamie's shoulders, and alternately spearing themselves through his short hair. He was making deep noises of pleasure and approval, not unlike when he ate something delicious. The sounds further amplified Rachel's arousal, and she had an almost overwhelming urge to ride the hard muscle of his thigh. Anything to assuage her mounting desire.

As if he knew what she wanted, Jamie intensified the kiss, licking deeply inside her mouth as he slid his hand over her hip and cupped her rear, urging her closer. Rachel complied, curling one leg around him as she pressed herself against his rigid length. Jamie gave a groan, and slid his hand inside the stretchy material of her bikini. He squeezed her buttock, his hand massaging the flesh and pushing her against his erection.

Rachel moaned softly, and reached between their bodies to cover him with her palm. Through the cool, wet material of his swim trunks, he was hard and hot.

She needed to touch him.

She quickly worked the lacings at the front of his trunks, and loosened them just enough to slip her hand inside. When she wrapped her fingers around his length, he jerked reflexively. He dragged his mouth from hers, and his breathing was ragged in her ear.

"God, that feels so good," he said hoarsely. "I want to be inside you."

His other arm came around her, lifting her into a better position. But without his free arm supporting them against the edge of the pool, they both sank below the surface of the water.

Rachel came up first, gasping for air. Jamie came up behind her, and pulled her toward the shallow end until their feet touched bottom. When she would have turned toward the steps that led out of the pool, Jamie caught her arm.

"Wait."

Rachel gave him a cautious look. His expression was taut, and beneath the clear waters she could see he was still aroused.

So was she.

If the water hadn't served to douse their rising passion, Rachel was certain she would have had sex with Jamie right there, in the pool, his broken leg be damned.

"I feel like I'm always apologizing," she said, her breathing still uneven.

"Then don't. The only thing I'm sorry for is letting go of the damned edge."

He gave her a lopsided smile and tugged at her until she stepped closer. She was careful to keep some space between them, and she fixed her attention on his face. No way was she going to look down at his broad chest, or his cobblestone abs, or lower to where his partially unlaced swim trunks were tented at an impressive angle.

"Jamie," she protested softly, seeing the expression in his eyes.

"What?" he demanded.

"We can't do this."

"Why not? We both want to."

"But it's not right."

"Why? Because you've decided it's not?" He tipped his head and looked into her eyes. "We're both free, consenting adults, Rachel. Who would we be hurting? Nobody."

"It's too soon." As excuses went, it was pretty lame.

"Really? Because you said you hadn't lived with Deke for almost two years. The marriage was over long before you got those divorce papers. So who's kidding who?"

Did Rachel want to drag Jamie out of the pool and finish what they'd started? Yes, badly. But she'd have regrets afterward. She couldn't remember the last time she'd slept with a guy for the sheer pleasure of it, without having the construct of a committed relationship. Had she ever? Maybe, once. When she'd been in college. And as much as she'd loved the sex, she'd hated the self-recrimination that came later. She wasn't like other women she knew, who fully embraced their own sexuality and pursued their own desires without guilt or worry. Besides being her brother's friend, he was her client. She wouldn't cross that line again.

"I can't, Jamie," she said now. "It has nothing to do with my not wanting to—I just *can't*."

"Can't?" he asked. "Or won't?"

Rachel tugged her arm free. "Does it matter?"

"Yes, damn it, it does matter."

Rachel gestured helplessly. "I won't have sex with a guy when I know there's no possibility of anything more."

"How do you know?" He held up a finger in warning.

"And don't tell me it's the age difference, because I'm not buying it."

"Look, Jamie," she entreated softly. "You're a great guy—really. You're gorgeous and you're smart, and any girl would be lucky to have you look twice at her."

"Just not you, huh?"

He sounded bitter and looked disappointed, and Rachel had the distinct impression it went deeper than just being told she wouldn't have sex with him. She'd let him down on some elemental level. But she couldn't tell him the truth—if she let her guard down and allowed herself to act on her feelings, their relationship could easily get out of control. She didn't want to risk falling in love with Jamie Colter.

He would only break her heart.

Chapter Eight

RACHEL DIDN'T GO over to Jamie's house the following morning to cook him breakfast. She didn't go over at lunch, and she didn't check to make sure he had everything he needed for dinner. In short, she spent the entire day avoiding him.

She'd thought she'd have the courage to take whatever he offered, but had quickly come to the realization she was a complete coward. She wouldn't make the same mistake she'd made with Deke. He'd also been a client, but she'd allowed herself to be flattered by his good looks and sweet words. She'd allowed herself to be swept away by his charisma, putting his needs before her own, doing whatever he asked of her until she'd lost her job, lost herself, and finally lost him.

Instinctively, she knew Jamie wasn't anything like Deke. He would never belittle or insult her. Instead, his eyes heated when he looked at her, and when he'd held her in his arms, she'd felt as if she was the most desirable woman on the planet.

And that was the problem.

How was she supposed to resist him, when every cell in

her body ached for his touch? She'd spent the entire night tossing and turning in her bed, recalling every luscious second of those moments in the pool. She remembered how hot and thick he'd been in her hand, and the deep, sexy sounds he'd made in his throat when she'd touched him. She could still feel the hard calluses of his palm on the bare skin of her bottom, and she'd wanted him to explore further.

Call her cowardly, but she couldn't face him. Not yet. Not until she got her own rioting emotions under control.

She peeked through the curtains at the house across the street for what seemed like the hundredth time that day, but there was no sign of Jamie. A wooden fence surrounded the backyard and concealed the pool area from view. Was he out there, lounging by the water? Was he angry with her? Did he even think of her?

Her phone rang, startling her, and she guiltily dropped the curtain back into place, even as hope flared it might be Jamie on the other end.

"Hi, Mom," she answered, after seeing the number on her display. "How's the cruise?"

"Wonderful. We just pulled into port at Maui today, and we finally have phone service again. How is everything going?"

Her mother's tone was cheerfully innocent, but Rachel knew better.

"Mrs. Colton talked with Jamie, didn't she?"

"She's concerned, since Jamie said he hasn't seen you yet

today."

"That's all he said?"

"I think so." There was a pause. "Why? Did something happen?"

Rachel walked into the kitchen, pulled out a stool and sat down. "No."

"So everything is fine?"

"Of course. Jamie's a big boy. If he needs me, he'll call."

"If you're sure..."

"I am. He doesn't need a nursemaid, Mom, and if there's an emergency then he has my number."

"But what if he's fallen? What if he's unable to call you?"

Rachel closed her eyes and counted to five, praying for patience. "You said he just talked to his mother. He's *fine*."

"Okay, if you're sure. But I think we'd all feel better if you just went over and checked on him. Not now, because that might seem suspicious, but maybe in a little while."

"Good night, Mom," Rachel said into the phone. "Enjoy Maui."

She could hear the smile in her mother's voice. "Goodnight, darling. Go check on Jamie."

Rachel hung up with a groan. If she didn't know better, she might just think her mother was doing a little old-fashioned matchmaking. Setting the phone down, she scrubbed her hands over her face and then looked at the clock. It was past eight o'clock, and her grumbling stomach reminded her she'd hardly eaten all day.

Now she stood up and opened the fridge to stare moodily at the shelves. Unlike Mrs. Colter, her own mother had not stocked the house with Rachel's favorite foods, and aside from the usual condiments, salad fixings, a half dozen eggs, and a chilled bottle of white wine, the shelves were mostly bare.

With a sigh, Rachel pulled the bottle of wine out and set it on the island. She was reaching for a wineglass when the doorbell rang. Frowning, she walked into the living room and peeked through the window. Jamie stood on the front steps, balancing easily on his crutches as he waited for her to answer the door.

Anticipation and dread warred inside her, and for a moment she actually considered not answering. As if sensing her watching him, Jamie looked toward the window where she stood, saw her peeking out, and gave a nod of his head.

Damn.

Drawing in a deep breath, Rachel quickly smoothed her hair and opened the door, determined to maintain a friendly, professional demeanor.

"Hi," he said, and gave her a rueful smile. "I come bearing gifts—sort of. Consider it a peace offering."

"Oh?"

Rachel tried to appear indifferent, which was difficult considering how good he looked. He'd managed to pull a pair of dark, loose sweatpants on over his cast, and wore a long-sleeved white T-shirt that hugged the planes of his chest and emphasized the breadth of his shoulders. The words *Virgin Islands* were printed on the length of one sleeve. That's when she realized he wore a backpack.

"So, are you going to make me stand out here all night, or can I come in? You know you want to know what I have in here."

Wordlessly, she stood back and let him in. He made his way to the kitchen and eased the backpack off, setting it on the surface of the island.

"Ah," he said, seeing the bottle of wine she'd left there. "Great minds think alike—I see we're on the same wavelength."

Setting his crutches aside, he eased himself onto a stool. Reaching inside the backpack, he drew out a bottle of red wine, and then a second bottle of white wine, along with two blocks of cheese and a box of crackers.

Rachel stood with her arms crossed. "You brought me wine and cheese."

"And crackers," Jamie added with a grin. "Since I haven't seen you all day, I thought maybe we could have a drink and swap stories about our day."

Rachel arched an eyebrow. "Okay. I sat on my butt all day and did nothing. You?"

Jamie laughed. "You're not getting off that easy." He twisted on his stool and glanced out through the sliding doors that led to the backyard. "I seem to recall your parents had a fire pit. Is it still there?"

"It is."

"Great. Why don't we move this party outdoors, and I'll get a fire going?" Without waiting for her response, Jamie stashed everything, including her bottle of wine, back into his backpack, and stood up. "Grab a couple of glasses, and a plate for the cheese and crackers."

Without waiting to see if she would do as he asked, he turned and made his way to the sliding doors. Shaking her head, but feeling inexplicably more cheerful, Rachel reached for two wineglasses and a small plate. Following Jamie outside, she set the dishware down on a small table. Unlike Jamie's backyard, which was dominated by the deck and swimming pool, Rachel's parents' yard was a profusion of lush gardens and flower beds bisected by meandering paths.

Closer to the house, there was a sunken, circular blue-stone patio with a stone fire pit in the center. Several chairs, including a double-chaise with matching side tables, had been artfully arranged around the pit and an overhead arbor had been strung with delicate fairy lights. The sun had already set, so Rachel flipped the lights on. The fire pit had already been set up for a fire, courtesy of Rachel's dad, so all Jamie had to do was ignite the fire starters that had been tucked beneath the stacked wood.

"There," he said in satisfaction, as flames started to lick at the edges of the wood. "That should get going in no time. Do you need a blanket?"

The temperature had dropped with the setting sun, and

Rachel realized it was fairly chilly outside. She wore a pair of jeans and a light top, and now she nodded. "Good idea. I'll just go grab one."

When she returned just a few minutes later, Jamie had opened the bottle of white wine and had poured them each a glass. Now he reclined on one half of the dual chaise with a pillow beneath his leg. He had the plate of cheese balanced on his thigh as he deftly sliced it into manageable pieces. He looked up as Rachel paused in the doorway to the patio, and patted the cushion next to him.

"C'mon and sit down. Don't be shy."

Rachel hesitated. Smart guy that he was, he'd chosen the only chaise that looked out over the shadowed gardens. Her choices were to sit next to Jamie in the twin chaise, or by herself on the far side of the fire. If she didn't sit with Jamie, she'd look like an uptight prude.

With as much nonchalance as she could manage, she settled herself onto the chaise next to him, and skootched herself back against the cushions. Then, unfolding the blanket she'd brought with her, she shook it out so it covered her legs.

"Do you want to share this with me?" she asked, knowing her tone was anything but gracious.

Jamie either didn't notice, or didn't care. "Sure," he replied, and pulled the extra material across his legs. He set the cheese plate down between them, and retrieved their glasses of wine from the side table, handing one to her.

"Cheers," he said, and tipped his glass against hers.

Rachel took a sip, enjoying the crispness of the wine, and then kept going, finishing the entire glass in one fell swoop.

"Okay, then," Jamie said, amused, and refilled her glass.

She watched the flames in the fire pit as they spread outward and grew larger, and she tried to pretend she wasn't acutely aware of the man seated next to her. A mere five inches of space separated their bodies, and he was so close she could actually *smell* him. By now, she was familiar with the scent of his soap and shampoo, and the underlying musk that was his alone. She breathed deeply, furtively.

"How long are you going to be mad at me?" he asked, idly turning the wineglass in one hand. Rachel watched, noting the strong, tapered fingers and neat nails. His hands fascinated her. She knew how they felt on her bottom. How would they would feel on the most sensitive parts of her body?

"I'm not upset with you," she said after a moment, and she realized it was true. In fact, she couldn't recall the last time she'd been this comfortable with someone, although that might have been the wine she'd just guzzled. She was beginning to feel the effects. Jamie was easy to be with. He made her laugh, and he had a way of putting her at ease so she felt she could say—and do—just about anything. And that was the problem. She'd allowed her guard to slip. She'd let herself forget he was her client. "I'm upset with myself."

Jamie swiveled his head to stare at her in surprise.

"Why?"

He was so close, even in the dim light from the overhead bulbs, she could see the faint bristle shadowing his jaw, and the strong vein that ran along the side of his neck and throbbed strongly. Rachel would only have to lean over to press her mouth against his skin.

"You know why," she said. "Because I forgot myself."

He looked at her with a mixture of exasperation and amusement and, reaching over, took her wineglass from her hand and set it down alongside his own.

"Come here," he murmured, and before Rachel could protest, he slid a hand along her jaw to cup her face and turn it for a kiss. Rachel didn't resist; if she was honest with herself, she'd been wanting this since she fled his house yesterday morning.

His mouth was warm and he tasted faintly of the wine, and the small sound of approval he made sent shivers of awareness along Rachel's spine. Almost without will, she leaned in to him. Her hand curled around his arm, feeling the muscles beneath the soft cotton of his shirt, and reveling in how solid and hard he was.

Jamie pulled back and studied her, before reaching up to smooth a stray tendril of hair back from her face. After a moment, a smile touched his mouth. "I want you to forget yourself, Rachel McCafferty."

"Rachel Narducci."

Jamie shook his head. "Nah, you're not a Narducci. Not

anymore."

Rachel smiled ruefully. "If I ever was. The more I think back on those days, the more I wonder why we got married in the first place."

Jamie shifted to look at her more fully. "That always did bug me. What was it about that dude that made you decide to go and marry him?"

His voice held so much contempt and disbelief that Rachel laughed. After a moment, she sighed, and shrugged. "I don't know. I was young and impressionable, and he was such a big personality. He used to call me doll-face, and even though it sounds old-fashioned, and maybe even a little condescending, I actually liked it." She risked a glance at Jamie. She'd never even told her girlfriends that bit, because she'd known how they would react. "Stupid, right?"

"To marry someone because he calls you doll-face?" Jamie made a scoffing sound. "Yeah." He picked up her hand in his and turned it over, before pressing a kiss against her palm, and then curling his fingers over it. "I would never call you doll-face. Sugar lips, maybe. Hot pants, definitely. Or maybe sweet cheeks."

Rachel snatched her hand from his, laughing in mock outrage. "Sweet cheeks?"

"C'mon," he teased. "You've got a great ass."

His compliment, however crude, made Rachel blush. Nobody—not even Deke—had ever told her she had a great ass.

"Thanks," she said with a grimace. "I think. But I didn't marry Deke just because he called me doll-face. For all his faults, he can actually be extremely charming, and when he turns his attention on you…" Her voice trailed off.

"You don't have to explain it to me," Jamie said. "I get it. The guy's a multi-millionaire, he's good-looking in his own bizarre, attention-grabbing way, and he probably showered you with gifts. How can anyone compete with that?"

His tone was one of frustrated resignation, and Rachel wondered if he might actually be jealous of Deke. She had been twenty-eight when she'd married Deke, who had been just twenty-five at the time. His family had been against the union, convinced Rachel was only after his money. Hence, the rigorous prenuptial agreement that had essentially denied her any portion of his wealth should they divorce without children.

But the truth was Rachel had been completely infatuated with Deke in those early years. He'd had a magnetism that drew you in and made you want to be close to him. Of course, his lavish lifestyle had been part of his allure. On their first date, he'd driven her to a local high school football field where a helicopter had been waiting. They'd flown to Martha's Vineyard for dinner, and had returned to LaGuardia Airport, where he'd handed her into his sports car and driven her home. She hadn't invited him up to her apartment that night, but she did the following night, and each night after.

But had she really loved him? She'd been hurt when the marriage had ended, but she hadn't been devastated. If she was honest with herself, she'd actually been a little relieved. Keeping up with Deke Narducci had been exhausting, both physically and mentally.

Deke had loved a good party, and had thought nothing of traveling halfway around the world to be part of a celebration. At first, Rachel had enjoyed accompanying him. Each party, each location had been more fabulous than the last. But eventually, she'd grown weary of the late nights, the constant travel, and the glamorous people. She wasn't in the same league as the other women at these social events, and she'd grown tired competing for Deke's attention. She'd started staying behind, letting Deke go alone. Maybe she'd been complicit in the death of their marriage, but looking back she realized it never would have lasted, no matter what she did.

"He could be pretty hard to resist," she agreed. "Unfortunately, he's the kind of guy who needs constant stimulation, and he becomes easily bored with the same thing."

Jamie stared at her in disbelief. "Are you seriously suggesting he became bored with you?"

Rachel shrugged one shoulder. "Apparently. He began cheating less than a year after the wedding. I didn't find out until much later, but that was his defense—he was bored."

"Not only is he a serious douche, but he also sounds like

a three-year-old."

Rachel laughed. "Yes, there are a lot of similarities between Deke and a toddler. But enough about him, okay? He's out of my life, and I'd just as soon not talk about him anymore. Could you hand me my wine?"

Reaching over, Jamie picked up the wineglass and handed it to her. "I don't know if this helps, but I always thought you were way too good for that guy."

"Thanks. I appreciate that." She took a long swallow of her wine. "Dylan said the same thing. He actually flew out to New York to try and change my mind about marrying Deke."

"Yeah, I remember. I even offered to pay his airfare if he succeeded in getting you to call the wedding off."

Rachel stared at him. "You knew about that?"

Jamie shrugged. "I may have encouraged him, a little."

"Was I the only one who didn't realize we were wrong for each other?" With a groan, she tipped the wineglass back and drained the contents, and then set the empty glass down on the patio beside the chaise. "Don't tell me any more; I don't want to know."

Reaching out, Jamie captured her free hand and laced his fingers with hers. "I'll just say one more thing," he said, "and then we'll never talk about the Deke-wad again."

Rachel looked at him, but there was no trace of laughter or mockery in his expression. Something inside her coiled itself in anticipation of what he might say, and she was acutely conscious of how warm and large his hand was.

"What's that?" she asked faintly.

"Deke is an idiot," he began, and his voice had a rough-soft quality that made Rachel's insides quiver. His gaze dropped to their linked hands. "Otherwise, he would never have let you forget how important you were to him, or how damned lucky he was to have you in his life. He'd have reminded you every day of how beautiful and special you are." He raised his eyes to hers. "And he damned sure never would have cheated on you."

"Jamie…"

Without conscious thought, she leaned toward him. Jamie released her hand and met her halfway, rolling toward her so he pressed her back against the cushions, bracing his weight on one elbow as he used his free hand to cup her jaw. His hair glinted gold in the firelight, and Rachel's eyes drifted closed in anticipation of his kiss. He traced his thumb along the line of her cheek before brushing it across her mouth. Without opening her eyes, Rachel lightly bit the pad of his thumb.

She heard Jamie give a small groan of surrender, and then he was kissing her, his lips pushing against hers until she opened willingly for the hot slide of his tongue. She speared her fingers into his short hair, urging him closer. He complied, slanting his lips over hers and licking at the inside of her mouth. He smelled delicious, and the warm, heavy weight of him against her breasts sent an ache of longing to her groin. She shifted slightly to accommodate him, and he responded by sliding his free hand to her breast.

Rachel gasped into his mouth as he cupped her gently, and then kneaded the flesh with his strong fingers. She hadn't been touched this intimately in a long time, and the sensations were almost overwhelming. When he brushed his thumb over her nipple, and then plucked at the sensitized bud through the fabric of her shirt and bra, she arched involuntarily, seeking more of the delicious contact.

"I want you to touch me," she breathed against his mouth.

"I am touching you," he said, laughing softly. "And you feel amazing."

In answer, Rachel covered his hand with hers, and brought it down to the vee of her legs where an insistent throbbing had begun the moment he began kissing her. He made a deep sound of approval and cupped her through the thin cotton of her pants, before rubbing his fingers along the seam of her sex.

Rachel realized her breathing had quickened, and she shifted her hips restlessly as he deepened the kiss. Her hand crept to his waist. More than anything, she wanted to touch him the way he was touching her. She could still recall how thick and hot he'd been when she'd touched him by the pool.

Jamie pulled away. His breathing was a little ragged, and even in the indistinct light, she could see the twin patches of hectic color high on his cheekbones.

"Sweetheart," he said, and his voice was a husky rasp. "We should probably move this indoors, where we can, uh—"

Looking down, Rachel saw the blanket had slid off. Beneath the soft sweatpants, Jamie was fully aroused, but was having difficulty getting into a comfortable position on the inclined chaise.

"Your leg!" Rachel exclaimed. "I'm so sorry! I wasn't even thinking—"

"Shh," he hushed her. "It's all good. I just think we should go indoors where we can get more comfortable."

"What about the fire?"

"Which one?" he asked, laughing and kissing her at the same time. He glanced at the fire pit. "I'll put the screen over the top. It'll be fine."

He eased himself away from her, and the cool evening air washed over Rachel's heated body, making her shiver. She immediately missed Jamie's solid weight and warmth. Pushing to a sitting position, she gathered up the blanket and their wineglasses, watching as Jamie eased himself to his feet.

He gave her an apologetic look. "If I could, I'd carry you inside. I don't want to stop touching you for even a second. Promise me this won't ruin the mood."

Rachel smiled. "It won't. In fact, I'll do the touching while we head inside."

If she was smart, she would take this opportunity to

change the direction of the evening, maybe even send him home. But her body still thrummed from his touch, and the sight of his arousal made her remember she was a woman, and she still had desires. So instead of doing the right thing and putting an end to the night, she waited while Jamie secured the fire pit, and then walked with him into the house, keeping one hand on his back as he swung his crutches. Once inside, she set the glasses and blanket down, and turned to Jamie.

"Where were we?" she asked.

Jamie moved closer to her, crowding her against the island. He supported his weight on one crutch as he slid a hand to the back of her head, gently tangling his fingers in her hair and tipping her face back.

"I'm crazy about you, Rachel McCafferty," he said softly, and lowered his mouth to hers. "I always have been."

Alarm bells rang in Rachel's head, but then he was kissing her, and she lost any ability to think coherently.

Chapter Nine

JAMIE NOTED WITH satisfaction Rachel didn't correct him on her surname. Instead, she wound her arms around his neck and kissed him, deeply. She tasted faintly of the wine they'd drunk earlier, and her body was warm and firm against his. She tangled her tongue with his, stoking his desire and causing a rush of heat straight to his groin.

Rachel pulled away and began pressing hot, wet kisses against his jaw and neck, even as her fingers slid beneath the hem of his shirt and pushed upward. Her hands were cool against his heated skin, and when she slid her palms over his abdomen, his flesh contracted beneath her touch.

"Everything about you is so hard," she murmured against his neck.

Oh, sweetheart, you have no idea.

He was stiff with arousal, and when her fingers dropped to the waistband of his sweats, he stopped her.

"Rachel, is there a couch or maybe even a bed we can use? I don't know how I'm going to do this with these damned crutches."

"I'm using the guest room," she said, and dropped her

hands from his body. "This way."

Jamie followed her through the house to a room beyond the living room. She switched on a small lamp and Jamie saw what had once been a playroom when they'd been kids was now a bedroom, complete with an attached bathroom.

"My grandparents can't really do the stairs anymore, so my parents converted this room to a bedroom," Rachel explained.

Jamie watched as she quickly gathered up some clothing she'd left on a nearby chair, and then flipped a small wireless speaker on, and soft music filled the air. Then she yanked the bedspread to the foot of the bed, and pulled the blankets back. He couldn't quite get his head around the unbelievable fact they were really going to do this. He was finally going to have sex with Rachel McCafferty and even if he couldn't last—and he was already so freaking aroused he doubted he could—it was going to be the most amazing two minutes of his life.

"Sit here," Rachel indicated, patting the edge of the bed. "I'm going to take care of you."

The way she said the words let Jamie know that taking care of him didn't have anything remotely to do with his injury. He eased himself onto the side of the bed, and dropped his crutches to the floor. He watched as Rachel stood in front of him and, never taking her eyes from his, she began to undress.

Slowly, as if wanting to torture him, she began to undo

the buttons on her blouse, her body undulating softy to the music. Her hair swirled around her shoulders in thick, glossy waves, and one long tendril fell over her eyes, giving her a sultry look.

Jamie's eyes were riveted to where her fingers were slowly unfastening the last button, and then spreading the edges of the blouse apart. Beneath the shirt, she wore a navy-blue lace bra. Beneath the open lace, he could see her pale skin and hints of her rosy nipples.

He swelled even more.

"Now it's your turn," she said, and moved forward so she all but straddled his good leg. She grasped the bottom of his shirt and tugged it upward. Jamie helped her by reaching behind his head and grabbing a fistful of the shirt, and pulling it off in one smooth motion.

"Lie back on the bed," she said, and pushed gently on his shoulders. Jamie complied, hitching himself back so he lay diagonally across the mattress. He watched as Rachel took a bed pillow and eased it under his cast to support his leg. "Is that good?"

Jamie was unabashedly admiring how the tops of her creamy breasts jiggled beneath the lace bra as she moved, and the only thing he could manage was a nod, and an incomprehensible mumble of assent.

"Good. Can you help me take these off?" She carefully climbed over his body to slide her fingers beneath the waistband of his pants.

Jamie complied by lifting his hips, and helping her push the fabric down. He'd forgotten he was going commando until she gasped softly, and the cool air wafted across his erection.

"Oh, Jamie," she whispered, and she stroked one fingertip along the ridge of his scar, where it curved downward and ended just above his groin.

"I got very, very lucky," he said. "I don't think I appreciated just how lucky, until right now." He took her hand and moved it to where he ached for her touch, and she complied, trailing her fingers oh-so-lightly along his length.

"You are so beautiful."

The awe in her voice, and her light touch caused his flesh to swell even more, and Jamie let his head fall back against the blankets as he struggled to breathe. She pulled the pants free of his legs, and he lifted his head to watch as she stripped her shirt off, and then reached behind her back to release her bra.

When the scrap of material fell away, Jamie sucked his breath in at the sight of the most perfect breasts he'd ever seen. Then she was unbuttoning her jeans and pushing them down over her hips and thighs, until finally, she wore nothing but a scrap of navy silk. Only then, when she saw him staring at her, did she look self-conscious. He could almost see her battling with the desire to cover herself, before she tipped her chin up and then came over him on her hands and knees, taking care to avoid his injured leg. Her breasts were right there, and it was all he could do not to haul her upward so he could bury his face between them.

She braced her hands on either side of his head and looked at him. Her hair curtained their faces, and Jamie resisted the urge to fist his hands in the luxurious mass and pull her down for his kiss. He sensed this needed to be done on her terms, so he remained still, while every cell in his body leaned forward, toward her.

"This is insane," she murmured softly, and ran the back of her finger along his jaw.

"Totally nuts," he agreed.

"I blame you." She drew her finger across his mouth, and down over his chin. "I blame your mouth, and the way you kiss, and that deep, sexy voice."

Jamie gave a huff of laughter. "I accept full responsibility, sweetheart. Just don't make me wait any longer. Kiss me."

To his relief, Rachel lowered her head and slanted her lips across his, feasting on his mouth as if she couldn't get enough. With a groan, Jamie slid his hands to her hips and then let them roam over her back, reveling in the satiny softness of her skin. Breaking the kiss, Rachel sat upright across his hips, and brought both his hands up to cover her breasts.

Jamie couldn't prevent his deep hum of pleasure and approval as he cupped and kneaded the pliant flesh. Her breasts were full and heavy in his hands, and when she arched her back, pushing them into his palms, he complied by squeezing them and then gently rolling her nipples between his fingers. Rachel covered his hands, encouraging him in his exploration.

Bending his head, he drew one tight nipple into his mouth and sucked on the small bud until she gasped and pushed his head away.

"It's too much."

"You feel so good," Jamie said. He loved the sight of her, nearly naked and straddling his hips. His hands were dark against the pale skin of her breasts. He could easily watch her all night. But when she shifted her weight to ride the rigid length of his cock, he didn't think he'd last very long. He could feel her heat and moisture, and the combination was almost more than he could stand.

"Here," he said, and shifted her slightly, sliding one finger inside the elastic of her insubstantial panties. "Take these off."

Rachel stared at him, and then attempted to pull the panties down without disturbing his leg. Jamie took the fragile material in his hands and ripped, and the panties came apart in his fingers, leaving Rachel completely naked.

"Sweet mercy," Jamie breathed, as Rachel gave him a sexy smile, and took him in her hand.

"Doing okay?" she asked softly, still smiling. Her hand slid over his length, and she smoothed her fingertips across the engorged head where a drop of moisture glistened.

Just seeing the dark triangle of hair above her cleft, and a hint of the soft folds hidden beneath was enough to push Jamie to the very brink. His balls ached, and he gritted his teeth, praying for the strength not to come before he was actually inside her.

"Baby," he groaned, "you are killing me."

Rachel laughed, and lowered herself so her breasts pressed against his chest. She kissed him sweetly, fusing her mouth against his.

"What is it you need?" she asked in his ear, and then traced her tongue across his jaw.

"You," he said against her lips. "Just you. Around me, surrounding me. Now."

"Do you have protection?"

For a moment, Jamie couldn't think clearly. Then her words sunk into his lust-sodden brain. "Yeah, in the pocket of my pants."

Rachel smiled against his mouth, and her teeth scraped lightly against his. "Pretty sure of yourself, huh?"

"Just hopeful," he corrected her.

He closed his eyes briefly, and focused on his breathing as she leaned to the side and reached down for his discarded sweatpants. Fishing in the pockets, she retrieved the sleeve of condoms he'd stashed there on his way out the door.

"Three!" she exclaimed. "I don't know whether to be flattered, or impressed."

"With you, three won't be enough," he managed to say.

Rachel tore one packet free and opened it with her teeth.

Jamie didn't think he'd ever seen anything as erotic as the sight of her rolling the latex over his penis, and the sensation of her hands gripping him firmly made him clench his teeth together.

"You don't have to do anything," Rachel said. "I don't want to risk hurting you."

"You won't," he assured her, his voice rough.

And then finally, she was easing herself over him, gasping lightly as she slid down his length. Jamie had to clench his back teeth hard as her slick heat gripped him, and then she was fully seated on him, her hands braced on his chest.

Jamie didn't think he'd ever experienced anything as incredible as Rachel surrounding him, and then she began to move. Her hair spilled over her shoulders and her beautiful breasts bounced gently with each movement. Jamie groaned loudly. He gripped her hips, but whether to slow her down or urge her on, he couldn't say.

"Jamie."

He looked up and saw she was watching him with an expression of intense arousal on her face. He thrust upward and she gave a small exhalation, and then bent forward, her hair draping around his face. Jamie cupped her face and drew her down and kissed her deeply, absorbing the taste, the feel, the sound of her.

Her inner muscles clenched around him, and he wasn't going to last. Dragging his mouth from hers, he made a guttural sound of pleasure. He was so damned close, but he didn't want to come without her.

"Sit up, baby," he said, his voice a harsh rasp.

Rachel complied, straightening, and then arched backward, slowly grinding her hips against his as her breasts thrust forward. She was achingly feminine, and Jamie didn't think he'd ever seen a woman as sexy or beautiful as Rachel McCafferty, riding his cock.

Jamie devoured the sight, but it only served to ratchet his lust higher. Reaching down, he pressed his thumb against the apex of her slick folds, feeling the hardened little nub beneath his finger. Rachel's face twisted, and she gave a broken cry of pleasure. She contracted around his length, again and again, and he watched her expression as she found her release, before he finally let himself go. He came in a white-hot rush, surging upward as he gripped her hips, pulsing deeply inside her until he was completely spent.

Rachel collapsed against his chest, and for a long time there was only the sound of their uneven breathing. After a few minutes, he withdrew carefully, and Rachel lay down beside him and put her head on his shoulder. She traced an invisible pattern across his torso with her fingertips.

"Was that good?" she finally asked.

Jamie angled his head to look at her in disbelief. He'd just had the most amazing, mind-blowing experience of his life, and she was asking if it had been *good*?

With a huff of laughter, he pulled her close and pressed his mouth against her hair.

"Sweetheart," he finally said, "if that had been any better, I'd be dead." He had a sudden, alarming thought. "Please tell me it was good for you, too."

Rachel started to laugh, and buried her face against his chest. When she looked at him, a smile curved her lips. "Are you kidding? I can't believe that's what I've been missing all these years."

Jamie sagged against the pillows in relief, even as he swelled with pride. He—skinny little Jamie Colter—had just made love to the girl he'd dreamed of for more than twelve years. Life couldn't get any better.

Chapter Ten

RACHEL DIDN'T KNOW how to tell Jamie that having sex with him had been a huge—scratch that, *colossal*—mistake.

All three times.

Closing her eyes, she groaned. What had she been thinking? The truth was, she hadn't been thinking. She'd had too much to drink. She could blame the wine, the firelight, and Jamie's proximity on the chaise as the reasons why her good sense had taken a vacation, leaving her with no ability to resist him.

But she'd be lying to herself.

Last night, she had wanted him.

Desperately.

But now, standing on the patio in the cool dampness of early morning with the acrid smell of ashes from last night's fire lingering in the air, it all seemed like a giant lapse in judgment. She'd come home to Glacier Creek to gain some perspective on her life—and on men in general. Jumping into the sack with the first good-looking guy who crossed her path was so not part of the plan!

But he was so unbelievably gorgeous!

And funny. And smart. And kind.

And hot.

Surely a woman could be forgiven for succumbing to the kind of temptation that was Jamie Colter. Rachel didn't know whether to despise herself for her lack of willpower, or fist-pump the air because she could still attract a good-looking, younger guy.

Oh, God, he was so much younger!

She definitely despised herself.

She obviously had no morals, and no discrimination, or she would never have allowed what was supposed to be a business relationship cross over the line into intimacy.

She was an idiot.

"Hey, what are you doing out here? I woke up to find you gone, and I had plans for you this morning."

Rachel turned to see Jamie standing just inside the sliding doors to the kitchen. At least he'd put his clothes on. She didn't think she could focus if he'd been bare-chested.

Ignoring the suggestion in his voice, she drew in a deep breath. "Jamie, we need to talk."

His face grew still. "Ah, here it comes. The little speech about last night being a mistake."

Rachel frowned. Was she that transparent?

"You have to know it was a mistake," she said, and pushed past him into the kitchen. She rinsed her cup in the sink—anything to avoid having to face him. "Last night was fun, but it can't happen again."

She didn't hear him come up behind her, and when she turned around he was right there. He crowded her against the counter, his expression intent.

"You're wrong," he said softly. "If anything, last night just confirms what I've suspected all along."

Looking into his eyes, Rachel was left breathless at what she saw reflected there. "What's that?"

"You and I are perfect together."

"Jamie—"

She tried to protest, but hitching his crutches more firmly beneath his arms, he cupped her face and kissed her, long and slow, until Rachel sighed softly into his mouth and leaned in to him. When he finally lifted his head, his blue eyes gleamed with satisfaction.

"Don't try to tell me that was a mistake," he murmured.

Rachel tried to clear the fog of desire that was quickly enveloping her. "Jamie," she persisted, and put her hands against his chest as if that might keep him away. "This isn't going to work. Yes, the chemistry is great, but I'm not the right woman for you."

Jamie gave her a tolerant look. "Please don't say it's the age difference."

"I wasn't, actually, but it's something you have to consider," she countered. "I'm thirty-three. Let's face it, the window on settling down and starting a family is closing."

Jamie looked at her then, and one eyebrow went up.

When he spoke, his tone was dry. "I don't recall asking you to marry me."

For just an instant, Rachel was too surprised to reply. Then she gave him a small shove, forcing him to step back. She slid out from between him and the counter and moved to the opposite side of the kitchen, putting the island between them.

"You're still my client."

"Technically, my parents are your clients," Jamie said. "I'm not paying you anything, so don't even try to use that angle. We're both adults. We can do whatever we want."

"So you're proposing a relationship based on sex?" she asked. She wanted to sound outraged, indignant, but knew her voice sounded more curious than anything else.

"We can start with that, if it makes you feel better."

"How is that supposed to make me feel better?"

Jamie grinned, unabashed. "Well, you said yourself the chemistry between us is great. I figure we can at least enjoy each other's company, and you don't have to feel any pressure that there's more to it than mutual pleasure." He shrugged. "If either one of us decides it isn't working, then we can go our separate ways as friends. No hard feelings."

Rachel narrowed her eyes at him, trying to decide if he was being sincere. His logic was incredibly tempting. She did enjoy his company, and the sex was off-the-charts incredible. Did she want a repeat of last night?

More than anything.

But Glacier Creek was a small town, and if word got out that they were hooking up, people would talk. Rachel didn't know if she could handle that. She'd been legally divorced for less than a week. She loved being with Jamie, but she wasn't naïve enough to think their relationship would last.

"What about you?" she finally asked.

"What about me?" He frowned.

"If we do this, and then I decide I want to move on, will you be able to accept my decision?"

He made a face as if to say that was a no-brainer. "Absolutely. Besides, I'm not going to be in Glacier Creek forever. As soon as I'm fit for duty, I'm heading back to California to rejoin my unit. I'll probably deploy again, which means I'm not going to be around for long myself."

Rachel considered him for a long moment. She wasn't sure she believed him, but suddenly she didn't care. Jamie made her feel sexy and uninhibited in a way she'd never felt with Deke. Maybe Jamie was just what she needed to restore her confidence.

"I do have one condition," Jamie said, before she could respond. She watched as he came around the island. Setting one crutch aside, he wrapped an arm around her waist and pulled her close, until her breasts flattened against his hard chest. "You are not allowed to talk about our age difference, because it's a non-issue. Agreed?"

She hadn't even agreed to his initial proposal, but found herself nodding.

"Agreed," she breathed.

"Good."

Dipping his head, he fused his mouth to hers. The kiss was designed to tempt and arouse, and it worked. Within minutes, much to her chagrin, Rachel was arching against him, pushing her fingers through his hair and demanding more. He smiled against her mouth before he dragged his lips along the length of her neck to nuzzle the sensitive spot just beneath her ear.

She shivered.

Jamie took her earlobe between his teeth and bit down gently. "I told you I had plans for you this morning," he said, his voice a husky promise in her ear.

Rachel gasped as he lifted the hem of the T-shirt she wore, and pushed her shorts and panties down around her thighs. Then his hand was there, exploring her damp heat until she moaned softly.

Before she realized what he was doing, he'd lifted her onto the island so the cool granite was beneath her bare bottom, and her legs dangled over the edge.

"Jamie! You're going to hurt yourself," she managed.

But it wasn't until he pulled up a chair, and eased himself onto it that Rachel understood his intent.

"Oh, no," she protested, her heart beginning to slam in her chest. "Not here."

"Oh, yes," he said, and slid her shorts and underwear completely off, as he slanted a wicked grin at her. "Here, and anywhere else we like, as often as we like."

Rachel knew she should jump down. She'd done some crazy things in her life, but sex on her mother's kitchen counter had never been one of them.

"Ohh..." she moaned in distress, seconds before Jamie's mouth touched her center. And when he positioned her legs over his shoulders and began to lave her with his hot, talented tongue, her moans turned to something altogether different, and any thought of denying him disappeared completely.

THE SUN WAS dipping behind the distant mountains, streaking the western skies with orange and pink, and taking the warm temperature of the day with it. Jamie sprawled in a lounge chair by the pool and watched Rachel as she dozed on the chair beside him. She wore a bikini top and a pair of shorts, and he watched the rise and fall of her smooth chest, recalling how her breasts had heaved with her agitated breathing earlier that morning, in the kitchen.

He'd lied when he'd told her they could have a no-strings-attached relationship. He'd been so worried she might end things right then and there, he would have said anything to persuade her to keep him around. The truth was, he was head over heels in love with her, and he had no intention of letting her go. In the few days they'd spent together, he'd rediscovered all the reasons why he'd been crazy about her. She was smart, funny, and easy to talk to. He'd even had tantalizing glimpses of the brashly confident girl she'd once been. He wanted that girl. She was in there, somewhere.

He loved watching her laugh, and thought he could easily spend the rest of his life coaxing that smile from her. Making love to her last night had just cemented the deal. It might take time before she finally realized he was the right guy for her—the only guy for her—but he had nothing but time on his hands right now. However long it took, he'd wait for her. Did he want to marry her? Oh, yeah.

He saw goose bumps rise on Rachel's skin, and squinted at the setting sun, which was almost completely gone now. The air was quickly growing chilly. Reaching out, he gently shook her awake.

"Hey, it's getting cold out here," he said, when she opened her eyes and looked at him in bemusement. "Let's go inside before you catch a cold."

She sat up and rubbed her hands over her arms. "You're right; I can't believe I fell asleep."

Jamie couldn't help feeling a little smug. "Well, you didn't get much sleep last night."

She actually blushed. "What time is it?"

"Almost seven. Getting hungry?"

"A little. What about you?"

"I'm always hungry." He laughed. "What if we head into

town and grab a bite to eat at Red's? I could go for some home cooking."

Red's Diner had been a fixture in Glacier Creek for as long as Jamie could remember, and he had a sudden hankering for their meat loaf and gravy. Rachel was fishing under the chair for her sandals and deliberately not looking at him.

"It's dinner, Rachel," he said, "not a marriage proposal. We both have to eat, and if I didn't have this goddamned cast on my leg, I'd drive myself into town. But I can't."

Rachel did look at him then, and he saw the apology in her eyes. "Right. Sorry. Red's sounds great."

"Why don't you go change into something warmer, and I'll do the same and meet you back here in fifteen minutes?"

"Do you, uh, need any help?"

Jamie grinned. "Sweetheart, I will never turn down an offer like that, but I should warn you—if you come anywhere near my bedroom, I guarantee we will not be heading into town for dinner."

Even in the fading light, Jamie didn't miss the warm color that crept into her face. She stood up reluctantly.

"In that case, I'll see you in a few minutes," she said.

Jamie watched her leave. She had regrets about sleeping with him, but he couldn't bring himself to sympathize. He had a short window of opportunity to prove to her just how perfect they were together, and he wasn't going to blow it.

RED'S DINER WAS comfortably busy, but they were seated at a booth near the windows right away. Rachel hadn't eaten at the diner in years, but it seemed nothing had changed in the time she'd been gone, except some of the wait staff were different. From where they sat, Rachel could see the length of Main Street all the way to the pier that extended out over the lake. Lights from the nearby homes and businesses reflected on the surface of the dark water. The shops on Main Street were still open, and the lights from the windows spilled onto the sidewalks as people strolled past. The scene was so different from New York City—with its congestion and overload of brilliant lights—that Rachel might have been on a different planet. She'd actually forgotten how beautiful Glacier Creek was at night, when she could see billions of stars glittering against the black velvet of the sky.

Everything was exactly the same as she remembered, and yet everything was completely different. Rachel turned her attention to the man who sat across the table, disconcerted to find him watching her over his menu.

"What are you thinking?" he asked.

"That Glacier Creek is more beautiful than I remembered," she replied. "Growing up, I couldn't wait to leave, and now I can't recall why."

"I get it." He peered out the window at the street. "There were times when I was over in Afghanistan or Syria, when thinking about Glacier Creek was what kept me going. When it was so freaking hot that your dog tags burned your skin, and the air inside the compound smelled like rotten onions, I'd think about the cool waters of the lake, and the snow on the mountains."

"If your leg prevents you from rejoining your unit, will you stay here?" she asked.

"Will you?" he countered.

She was prevented from answering by the approach of a waitress, and then the moment was gone. Jamie ordered a beer and a plate of meat loaf with mashed potatoes and gravy, while Rachel opted for a glass of white wine, and fresh lake trout with a green salad.

She sipped her wine and watched the other patrons in the diner, recognizing several of the faces, but not recalling their names.

"We could take a stroll onto the pier after dinner," Jamie suggested, pulling her out of her thoughts.

"That sounds nice," Rachel agreed. "Your chair is in the back of the van."

Jamie made a groaning sound and tipped back in his chair. "I can't wait to get this damned cast off. At least get one that lets me bend my leg."

"That's happening next week, isn't it?"

"Yeah, at my appointment with the surgeon at the VA in Kalispell." He gave her a lopsided smile. "You still going to drive me there?"

"Of course! That's what I'm getting paid for."

There was an uncomfortable silence as Jamie regarded

her quizzically, and Rachel realized how insensitive her words sounded. "I mean, I would drive you regardless," she amended.

"Sure." Jamie sounded unconvinced, and then their food arrived.

Rachel watched as he dug into his meal, but he didn't seem to relish his food, and there were none of the usual sounds of appreciation as he ate. Feeling as if someone had just stepped on her heart, Rachel picked at her trout, her appetite gone.

"Ms. Narducci?"

Rachel looked up to see a man standing by their table. He wore the uniform of a Glacier Creek firefighter, and her heart did a quick double-beat.

"Yes?"

"Uh, hello ma'am. I'm Scott Ross, and I work over at the Glacier Creek firefighting base." He was young, probably no older than Rachel, with dark hair and eyes, but she didn't recognize him. He looked both uncomfortable and distressed. "I'm sorry to disturb your dinner, but I thought you'd want to know—"

"Is it Dylan? Is he okay?"

Rachel saw by the expression in the man's eyes she was right, and he confirmed it when he gave a curt nod of his head.

"Yes, ma'am. He was injured during a jump, and was airlifted to a trauma center in Bozeman this afternoon. We tried to call your parents, but there was no answer so we left a voicemail message."

"What are his injuries?" This from Jamie, whose entire demeanor had undergone a drastic change when Scott Ross began to talk. He was on full alert and looked more serious than Rachel had ever seen him. Just seeing his somber expression made her aware of the severity of the situation.

"I don't have the details on his condition," Scott replied. "I only know he's busted up pretty good." He handed Rachel a slip of paper. "Here's the name and address of the hospital where they brought him, and that's the name and number of our captain. He's still on the front line of the blaze, but I think he's planning to get over to the hospital as soon as he can."

A wave of fear washed over her. She hadn't seen Dylan in over a year, but she loved her brother and dreaded the thought of anything happening to him.

"How did you find me?" she asked.

Now the firefighter looked embarrassed, and his gaze flicked uncomfortably between her and Jamie. "Some folks have seen you out together, and—well, it's a small town. I saw the van parked in the handicapped spot outside, so I figured you might be in here."

"Yes, well," Rachel didn't look at Jamie, "Mrs. Colter hired me to help Jamie—drive him around and do errands for him—while she and her husband are on a cruise with my parents."

Rachel knew she sounded prudish, but she suddenly couldn't bear the thought of the townspeople thinking she and Jamie were an item, not when most people didn't know about the divorce and likely thought she was cheating on her husband. Sleeping with Jamie was one thing, but she hadn't counted on their relationship becoming public knowledge. They'd only come into town together once, yet that had been enough for people to take notice and draw assumptions. Never mind they had been correct. The last thing she wanted was for people to think she'd found herself a boy-toy.

"Ah." Scott Ross rocked back on his heels and looked thoughtful. "That must be why we couldn't reach your folks. Sometimes those cruise ships don't get good wireless reception."

Rachel focused on the slip of paper he'd handed her. "Thank you. I'll call the hospital now and find out what's going on." She rose to her feet and glanced at Jamie, whose expression was inscrutable. "I'll be right back."

When she returned ten minutes later, the table had been cleared and Jamie had paid the bill.

"How is he?"

"He's in surgery right now. He shattered a kneecap and he has a ruptured spleen."

"But he'll be okay?"

Rachel nodded. "Yes, thank goodness."

"That's good news," he said. "He's in good hands, and there isn't anything you can do for him right now, so try not to worry. Why don't we go home and pack a bag?"

Rachel nodded. "Yes, okay."

In the van, on the way home, Rachel risked a glance at him in the rearview mirror, unsettled by his silence.

"Are you okay?" she ventured.

"Oh, are you talking to me?" he asked, and she heard the mild sarcasm in his voice. "I mean, I'm surprised, since you're only here to drive me around and run errands for me."

Rachel gave him a tolerant look. "That's not what I meant, and you know it. But I was hardly going to let him assume we're—that we're *dating* or something. I mean, how would that look?"

Jamie didn't answer.

"You have to admit if people knew we were hooking up, they would look at us with raised eyebrows," she persisted. "Most people have no idea Deke and I are divorced. There would be talk."

Jamie made a scoffing sound. "Those would be your own insecurities talking. I doubt anyone thinks long enough about either of us to even give it a second thought."

Rachel had her doubts, but she didn't want to argue with him. "I have to get a call through to my parents," she said, changing the subject. "I have an emergency number my mother gave me, then I'll head down to Bozeman. If I leave within the next hour, I can probably be there by midnight."

"I'm coming with you."

Rachel glanced at him in the mirror, surprised. "You don't have to do that."

"Dylan is my best friend," Jamie reminded her. "You don't think I'm going to let you go down there alone, do you?"

Rachel had been so wrapped up in her own thoughts and fears that for a moment she'd completely forgotten Jamie and Dylan were buds. Of course he would want to go down to Bozeman with her.

"But your leg—"

"I'll be fine. The van is comfortable, and I'd feel better if I went with you." He snorted. "At least then I won't lie awake wondering if you're okay, or if you fell asleep and drove off the road."

"I will not drive off the road."

"No, you won't, because I'll be with you to keep you awake."

Rachel refocused her attention on the road, refusing to admit even to herself how much she liked the sound of that.

Chapter Eleven

THE DRIVE TO Bozeman went faster than Rachel had anticipated, and it all had to do with Jamie. As the van swallowed up the miles and the dark road flew beneath the wheels, he kept up a steady, humorous dialogue, so she was hardly aware they had been driving for over three hours until suddenly, there was the sign indicating they had crossed into Bozeman.

"We're here!" she exclaimed in surprise.

"You did good," Jamie replied from the back row. "It's just past midnight. What do you want to do first—head over to the hospital, or grab a room somewhere and catch some sleep?"

That made Rachel pause. Just the thought of spending the night with Jamie caused heat to pool in her center. She decided she really was a terrible person, because she was already looking forward to spending time with him in Bozeman, where nobody knew either of them, and nobody would judge them.

"I'd feel better if we could check in on Dylan first," she said, glancing at Jamie in the mirror. "I told my parents I would call them as soon as I had talked with the doctor. Hawaii is four hours behind us, so they'll still be up and waiting to hear from me."

"The hospital it is, then," Jamie said.

They pulled into the dark parking lot fifteen minutes later, and Jamie eased himself into his wheelchair. They made their way to the patient information desk, where a nurse asked them to wait in a nearby lobby for Doctor Hartmann.

The hospital was eerily quiet, but there was one other occupant in the small waiting area. A man sat on the opposite side of the room, his head bent into his hands. He wore a heavy yellow shirt and a pair of military fatigue pants, both of which were dark with dirt and soot. On the floor beside him was a red backpack and a firefighter's hard hat. Rachel exchanged a meaningful look with Jamie.

"Excuse me, sir?" she ventured.

The man raised his head, and Rachel was momentarily taken aback by the red-rimmed, bloodshot eyes in the soot-darkened face.

"Yes?"

"Did you come in with Dylan McCafferty?" Rachel asked.

He straightened. "I did, yeah. And you are—?"

Rachel extended her hand. "I'm his sister, Rachel, and this is his good friend, James Colter. We came as soon as we got the news."

The man stood up and shook both of their hands. He was tall and lean, and beneath the dust and grime, very good-looking. "I'm Tyler Dodson."

"How is he?" Jamie asked.

Tyler's eyes swept over Jamie, taking in the wheelchair and extended cast on his leg. "He got caught in a crosswind during a jump and came down in a copse of trees. His leg is busted up pretty good, and he was impaled on one of the tree branches."

Rachel gasped, her hands flying to her mouth. "Oh my God," she breathed. "I didn't know…"

Tyler looked grim. "The doc said they'll need to remove his spleen, and he'll be laid up here for a week, at least."

"Have you seen him?" Rachel asked. Jamie had rolled his chair closer to her side, and now he reached out and took her hand in his. Rachel didn't pull away, drawing strength from his presence.

"No, he's still in surgery. I'm just waiting for the doc to come out and give me an update." His bleary gaze shifted beyond them. "There he is now."

Both Rachel and Jamie turned to see a surgeon, still wearing his scrubs, walking toward them. His face was somber, but he gave them a weary smile.

"You're Mr. McCafferty's sister?" he asked, extending his hand. "I'm Peter Hartmann."

"How is he doing?"

"Your brother is strong. He came in with an open fracture of the kneecap. Essentially, the patella shattered and we had to perform surgery immediately since he had bone fragments that perforated the skin. We also removed his spleen, but I expect him to make a full recovery."

"Can I see him?"

The doctor hesitated. "He's still in recovery and pretty groggy. You can see him, but only for a moment."

Rachel nodded. "I'll be quick."

"I'll stay here," Jamie said, releasing her hand. "I'll have a chance to see him tomorrow, when he's a little more lucid."

"Do you mind if I tag along?" Tyler asked. "I'd like to be able to tell the captain he looks better than he did when we pulled him out of that tree."

Leaving Jamie in the waiting area, Rachel followed Doctor Hartmann through the corridors, as Tyler Dodson walked quietly alongside.

"Are you going back to the wildfire?" she asked him.

He nodded. "Yeah. I'll head back to the base camp tonight. The captain will likely come by in the next day or so to check on him." He slanted her a questioning look. "How long are you planning to stay in Bozeman?"

"My parents are on a cruise in Hawaii, and I'm not sure when they'll be able to make it back here. We'll stay here until they arrive."

"You and James."

He said it as a statement, and although she didn't detect any judgment in his tone, Rachel couldn't help but feel defensive. "Yes. Jamie grew up across the street from us. He's Dylan's best friend."

"Yeah, I got that," he said. "I just thought you two were—" He broke off. "Never mind, I haven't gotten more than four hours of sleep in the past three days, so I'm a little out of touch with reality."

"No, tell me," Rachel urged. "What did you think?"

Beneath the soot and dirt, Rachel thought she saw a flush darken his cheekbones. "It's none of my business, but I thought maybe you were a couple." He shrugged. "If you're not, my mistake."

Before Rachel could respond, they reached a set of swinging doors, and Doctor Hartmann held them open. "He's through here," he said, indicating a room filled with medical monitors, and beds partitioned by curtains. He stopped at the end of one bed, and Rachel couldn't contain her soft gasp when she saw her brother.

One leg lay cushioned on a foam pad, with ice packs on either side of the knee. The knee itself had ballooned to three times its normal size, and a long incision ran over the top, closed with surgical staples. To Rachel, it looked like something out of a horror movie. The leg itself was swollen and discolored, and several other wounds had also been closed with staples.

He was covered with only a light sheet. Rachel could see tubes protruding from his abdomen, and his entire torso was mottled with darkening bruises. Her brother's dark blond hair, which normally hung to his shoulders in careless waves, was hidden beneath a surgical cap. Only the dark scruff of beard growth on his face looked familiar to Rachel.

"He looks worse than he is," Doctor Hartmann assured her. "I'll let you visit for a minute, but keep it brief."

Rachel nodded, her eyes on Dylan. "Of course."

She moved to the side of his bed and, careful not to disturb the intravenous tubing in his arm, took his hand in hers. She studied his face, noting the changes since she'd last seen him. With his strong jaw, chiseled cheekbones, and golden good looks, he'd never had a shortage of girlfriends. The few people who'd made the mistake of thinking his long hair meant he was a tree-hugger didn't know the real Dylan McCafferty. He was an adrenaline junkie; an extreme adventurer always in search of the next thrill. He was happiest when jumping out of a plane or battling a wildfire. Now she looked at his leg. Would he ever jump again?

"He'll be okay," said Tyler. "It'll be a good three to six months before he can resume normal activities. I doubt he'll ever jump a fire again, but considering he could be dead, I think that's a preferable alternative."

Rachel nodded and blinked back sudden tears. "All he ever wanted was to be a smoke jumper."

Beside her, Tyler laughed softly. "Not to argue, but I don't think that's entirely true. All Dylan wants is a challenge. Tell him he can't do something, and guaranteed he's going to find a way to get it done."

Rachel smiled. "That's true. I remember when he was training for the fitness test. He'd run up a mountain with a seventy-pound pack on his back every morning, and it wasn't enough to just beat the time, he had to kill it."

"That's Dylan," he agreed, and then suppressed a yawn. "I don't know about you, but I'm beat. I'm going to head back to the base camp and try to get a few hours of sleep."

Leaning down, Rachel pressed a kiss against her brother's face. Then, with one last look at him, she followed Tyler back to where Jamie waited for them in the lobby.

"Where do you want to stay?" he asked, after they left the hospital and he had settled himself into the back of the van. "We passed a bunch of hotels downtown."

"I made reservations at a lodge on the outskirts of town," Rachel replied. "It looked nice, and the rooms are big."

There was a momentary silence. "You already made reservations?" Rachel heard the disbelief in Jamie's voice. "When did you do that?"

"While I was packing my overnight bag to come down here." Rachel pulled out of the hospital parking lot and onto the main road, suddenly aware of how tired she was. "You forget; this is my specialty. I have two dozen travel agents on speed dial, so booking a place in Bozeman was a cinch."

"A lodge, huh?"

She glanced at him in the rearview mirror. "There's some kind of big rodeo going on through the weekend, and a lot of the downtown hotels are fully booked. This place sounds nice, and we'll only be here until my parents arrive."

"One room?"

Rachel smiled. "Of course."

"Then I'm going to love the place."

The sprawling wilderness-style lodge overlooked a river, and was constructed of massive logs with a steeply peaked center roof that soared four stories high. Jamie eased himself into his wheelchair and stacked their two duffel bags onto his lap, before expertly wheeling himself up the ramp and through the wide entry doors.

Inside, Rachel stopped for a moment, and just stared in awe at their surroundings. A massive waterfall, complete with rock formations, trees, and other greenery, dominated the center lobby, while the ceiling soared upward. On the far side of the lobby was an enormous stone fireplace flanked by live pine trees. Looking up, Rachel saw each level of the hotel had a balcony that overlooked the lobby, supported by immense tree trunks. Tables with colorful umbrellas were arranged around the waterfall, and a gurgling stream meandered through the lobby, crisscrossed by rustic footbridges. Deer heads had been mounted on the supporting pillars, and chandeliers made of antlers hung suspended over the tables and the reception desk.

"Wow, this is pretty spectacular," Jamie commented.

"I like everything except the animal head display," Rachel said, wrinkling her nose. "All those eyes watching me..." She shivered.

Jamie nodded. "Yeah, I have to agree with you."

They checked into their room, and made their way to the third floor. As they passed through the hallway, they were on eye-level with the top of the waterfall, and Rachel saw the lobby ceiling was a glass dome, through which she could see the stars.

Inside their room, Jamie tossed their bags onto a chair, and swiveled around, taking in the king-sized bed, the sitting area complete with small kitchenette, and the sliding doors that led to a private balcony.

"Well, at least there are no prying eyes in here," he commented.

"Yes, thank goodness," Rachel agreed. She pushed her hands through her hair. "I'm just going to brush my teeth and freshen up before bed."

Jamie nodded. "Sounds good."

In the bathroom, she almost wailed with despair when she saw her reflection in the mirror. Her hair had mostly come loose from the ponytail, and hung in messy disarray around her face, which looked pale and tired.

Shedding her clothes, she turned on the shower and then coiled her hair into a bun on top of her head, before stepping beneath the hot spray of water. The day's tension eased from her body, and she spent several long minutes under the stream, letting the hot water soothe her troubled thoughts. She dried off quickly and pulled on a pair of boxer shorts and a T-shirt, before letting her hair down and using her fingers to fluff it around her face. She quickly brushed her teeth, and then pinched some color into her pale cheeks.

Drawing a deep breath, she opened the door to see Jamie was already in the big bed. His toiletries sat on the counter beside the kitchenette sink, and his clothes were folded on a nearby chair. He'd turned the bedside light on to the lowest setting and the room was cast in shadows, but Rachel could see he was asleep, and she felt a pang of guilt for having kept him up so late. Careful not to disturb him, she slid beneath the sheets, and reached out to turn off the light.

In the darkness, she could just make out his profile, and the steady rise and fall of his chest. He wasn't wearing a shirt, and Rachel cautiously snuggled against him. She slid a hand over his chest, feeling the warmth of his skin and the contour of the muscles beneath. She wanted to slide her fingers lower to explore the hardness she'd glimpsed earlier, but was reluctant to disturb him. She closed her eyes, pushing down her disappointment.

JAMIE LAY AWAKE for a long time after Rachel crawled into bed beside him. He could smell the clean, floral fragrance of the soap she'd used, and when she slid her hand over his bare skin, his body reacted instantly. He'd had to stifle his groan of frustration and concentrate on keeping his breathing even, knowing if she slid her hand downward, she'd discover he wasn't asleep at all.

Far from it.

More than anything, he wanted to lift her over him and have her straddle his aching body; to bury himself inside her and lose himself in her tight heat. But he recalled again the weariness in her eyes and the exhausted slump of her slender shoulders. She needed sleep more than he needed sex.

Grateful when she curled on her side, he listened to her breathing grow slower, until finally she was asleep. He blew out a hard breath and flung one arm over his head, staring through the darkness at the ceiling, knowing he wouldn't find sleep quite so easily.

HE COULDN'T SEE anything. Couldn't move. Could barely breathe for the thick dust and grit that filled his nostrils and mouth.

He lay in utter blackness, pinned where he was by the weight of the heavy concrete above him. When he tried to shift, agonizing pain tore through him, as if someone had taken a red-hot poker and driven it through his midsection.

Somewhere, in the darkness, he heard a tortured moan. Someone was dying, and there wasn't a fucking thing he could do to help. Was it Santos? He tried to call his buddy's name, but when he opened his mouth, it filled up with dirt until he began to choke.

He was being strangled.

He was dying.

He struggled to free himself, but he couldn't move.

Someone called his name.

"Jamie. Jamie."

His lifeline. His only hope.

"Jamie."

A hand touched his shoulder, and he surged upward on one elbow, disoriented and gasping for breath.

"Jamie, you were dreaming, but you're safe now."

He turned his head and realized he was in bed with Rachel. She had turned on the bedside lamp and now she leaned over him on one elbow, her face clouded with concern. He shoved a hand through his hair, trying to dispel the nightmare. Outside the window, the sun had already risen.

"Water," he managed to croak.

Without hesitation, Rachel jumped out of bed and hurried over to the sink, filling a tall glass with water and carrying it back to him. She knelt on the mattress beside him as he drank it in noisy gulps. He swore he could still feel the grit of the nightmare in his throat.

He handed Rachel the empty glass and fell back against the pillows. He was coated in a fine sheen of sweat, and he felt weak, as if he'd just completed a triathlon.

"Hey." Rachel smoothed a cool hand over his brow. "Are you okay? Do you want to talk about it?"

"No," he said, his voice a harsh rasp. Reaching out, he pulled her down beside him and wrapped his arms around her, breathing in her soapy-clean scent. She represented everything that was good and pure, and right now he needed that. He wanted to lose himself in that with an urgency that wouldn't be denied.

Reaching down, he began pushing her boxer shorts down over her hips. "Take these off," he muttered, too impatient to have any finesse.

She did as he asked, shimmying out of the boxer shorts, and then pulling her T-shirt over her head until she was completely nude. He devoured the sight of her slender curves, her full, high breasts with their dusky tips, and the thatch of dark hair between her legs. Without waiting to be asked, she leaned over him and pulled his shorts down over his hips, easing them over his cast until she could pull them free.

He was already hard, his erection straining against his stomach. He didn't want to wait; he *couldn't* wait. He needed to be inside her *now*.

"Hurry," he demanded.

Rachel raised one leg to straddle his hips, and he moistened his fingers with his tongue and swiped them over her cleft in a crude effort to prepare her. Then he grasped her hips in both hands and surged upward, pushing himself into her hot, tight depths with a loud groan of satisfaction.

Rachel gasped, and then she was working with him,

rocking her hips and clenching her inner muscles with each forceful thrust. Lust swirled through him and the nightmare receded. He'd been prepared to reach his own climax without her, but watching her as she rode him, he realized she was close. Her face tightened in an expression of pleasure-pain as she neared her climax.

Jamie watched as her orgasm rolled over her, and then he let himself go with a guttural cry of release, surging upward as she tightened around him, pouring himself into her until there was nothing left for him to give.

Chapter Twelve

THEY DIDN'T TALK about the nightmare or the sex, but the experience left Rachel shaken. Jamie had disappeared into the bathroom immediately after; there had been no cuddling or pillow talk. Rachel lay in bed, listening to the water run, reliving those urgent moments. She had never, ever been used so thoroughly, or enjoyed it so much. She only wished the catalyst for the desperate coupling had been different.

She recalled again the sound of Jamie's moans as he'd been caught in the grip of his nightmare. She hoped never to hear those sounds again. They'd terrified her, made her want to weep for what he'd been through. When he emerged from the bathroom, showered and dressed, he'd once again donned the persona of the audacious, teasing lover and any chance to ask about what had happened was gone.

They ate a quick breakfast in the majestic lobby of the lodge, sitting at the foot of the waterfall, and then they headed back to the hospital. Now they stood outside Dylan's room as the doctor finished his morning examination.

"How is he?" Rachel asked, when the doctor and a nurse

emerged from the room.

"I'd say he's much better," Doctor Hartmann replied, jotting notes onto a clipboard. He looked at Rachel and grinned. "He's asking how long before he can jump again."

Rachel smiled. "That sounds about right. Is it okay if we go in?"

"Of course."

Dylan had his eyes closed, but he opened them when he heard their approaching footsteps, and his expression immediately transformed into a smile of welcome.

"Hey! This is a surprise!"

To Rachel, his voice sounded weak, but he looked much better than he had the previous day. He'd removed the green surgical cap, and now his hair spilled around his face in the glorious honey-brown waves that had driven girls wild for as long as Rachel could remember.

"Don't try to sit up," she advised, as she bent over and kissed his cheek. "I came as soon as I heard."

Dylan gave her a weak grin, and rubbed his fingers along the scruff on his jaw. "If I'd known you were coming, I'd have cleaned up. And where'd you pick up this loser?" He lifted a hand and fist-bumped Jamie, who had moved to the opposite side of the bed. "Jesus, man, you look like shit."

Jamie laughed. "Yeah, well have you looked in a mirror? I know you've always been jealous of me, but did you really have to jump into a tree just to one-up me? Looks like you're going to have a pretty impressive scar to show off to the ladies."

Dylan gave a dramatic groan. "Man, that wind caught my chute and I was like dandelion fluff, going whichever way it blew me."

Rachel took his hand. "You're lucky to be alive."

Dylan was silent for a moment, and Rachel knew he was thinking about his former boss, who had been killed in an accident eerily similar to his own a few years earlier. Then he seemed to give himself a mental shake, and shifted his gaze to Jamie.

"You doing okay, bro? I tried to come see you, right after they shipped you home, but the timing didn't work out. I got called up for a wildfire in Alaska, instead."

Jamie shrugged. "I can't complain. I have a follow-up appointment with the surgeon early next week, and hopefully they'll take this off and transition me to a boot." He grinned and nodded his head toward Rachel. "And I have this one here taking excellent care of me."

Dylan looked bemused. "Yeah, how the hell did you two hook up?"

Rachel's gaze sharpened on her brother. Did he suspect she and Jamie were more than just neighbors?

"Mom and Dad are on their annual cruise with the Colters," she reminded him, "so they asked me if I would mind helping him out while they're gone."

Dylan frowned. "So you're home now? Why didn't anyone tell me?"

"It was a last-minute decision." She pulled her hand free from Dylan's and focused on removing an invisible bit of lint from her jeans. "Deke and I are officially divorced, and I just needed to get out of New York."

"About damned time," Dylan said darkly. "I always hated that prick. You should have listened to me when I told you not to marry him."

Rachel gave him a weak smile. "Well, you were right."

"So what are you going to do now?" he asked. "Not a lot of potential clients in Glacier Creek, although we do have seasonal residents with a lot of dough. Maybe Lucas can hook you up with some of them."

Rachel vaguely remembered Lucas Talbot, the third friend in her brother's childhood trio. He lived on Long Island, but had spent his summers in Glacier Creek, since his billionaire stepfather had owned a luxury mountain home overlooking Flathead Lake. The three of them had been inseparable every summer when they were growing up. She recalled Lucas's family had even paid for Dylan and Jamie to accompany them on several ski vacations to Europe.

Now her eyes flicked to Jamie. "Thanks, but I don't know how long I'll be in Glacier Creek. I was thinking maybe I'd start my own business in California."

"Really." Dylan's voice held surprise and skepticism. "And that would be as a personal assistant?"

"A personal concierge," she corrected him.

Dylan looked puzzled. "Is that even a real thing?"

Jamie laughed. "That's exactly what I said!"

Rachel raised her hands in surrender. "I give up. Yes, it's a real thing, but you wouldn't know because you lack the kind of money it takes to afford one."

Dylan snorted. "Don't you mean I lack the kind of temperament to need one? I refuse to ask other people to do what I can do for myself."

Rachel looked meaningfully at his leg, swollen and bruised and held together with staples. "Okay. Well, let me know how that works out for you."

But Dylan only laughed, and then groaned as the movement caused pain to his abdomen. Rachel immediately regretted teasing him.

"Can I do something for you? Do you need pain meds?"

But Dylan only shook his head. "No, it'll pass. I'm trying not to dope myself up."

"Why would you allow yourself to be in pain?" Rachel asked. "Honestly, do you have to be macho *all* the time?"

Dylan actually looked embarrassed. "Captain Gaskill—my boss—called to say he'll be stopping by later today, and I'd like to be coherent."

"When are they going to let you out of here?" she asked, changing the subject.

"Maybe another week." He indicated his knee. "They have to wait for the bones to knit, and make sure an infection doesn't set in."

"So then you can return to Glacier Creek?" she asked.

"That's the plan."

He closed his eyes, effectively dismissing her. Rachel exchanged a look with Jamie. Dylan might fool some people with his brash confidence and free-spirited lifestyle, but Rachel knew him a little better than that. He had his own place on the outskirts of Glacier Creek, and he'd rather be there than in Bozeman. He probably didn't want to acknowledge he might be stuck here for a week or more.

"Hey," she said, and touched his arm.

He cracked one eye open and looked at her.

"Is there anything you need? Jamie and I are going to let you get some rest, but we can come back in a few hours. What do you want us to bring you?"

"A fifth of Jack Daniel's, a cheeseburger, and a curvy blonde," he quipped.

"I might be able to do the burger," Rachel said with a smile, "but you're going to have to wait on the other two."

He tried to shift to a more comfortable position and grimaced in pain as he did so. Rachel noted the lines of strain on either side of his mouth. She pushed herself to her feet.

"We're going to go now, but we'll come back later," she said. "If you're not going to take any pain meds, at least try to get some rest before your visitors arrive."

Dylan looked over at Jamie. "Can you hang back for a minute?"

"Yeah, sure," Jamie agreed.

Rachel paused at the foot of Dylan's bed, but when both

men gave her an expectant look, she rolled her eyes. "Fine, I get it. I'll be in the main lobby."

She waited for Jamie by the main entrance, trying not to think about what they could be discussing. Had Dylan wanted to drill Jamie on why they were together? Did he suspect they were sleeping together? Despite the fact Dylan was six years her junior, he'd become more protective of her as he'd grown older, and he'd never made any pretense of the fact he disliked her ex. So while Dylan might be happy about her recent divorce, that didn't mean he'd be thrilled about her hooking up with his best friend.

Fifteen minutes later, she watched as Jamie rolled his chair toward her through the corridors. As he drew closer, he slid his sunglasses on, effectively hiding his eyes.

"Ready?" he asked.

"Is everything okay?"

Jamie nodded. "Yup. Fine."

Without saying any more, he hit the handicap button beside the door and when they slid smoothly open, he rolled through without waiting to see if Rachel followed him. She stared after him, dumbfounded, then marched after him.

"You're seriously not going to tell me what Dylan wanted to talk to you about?" she demanded, catching up with him.

"Just guy stuff," he said. "No big deal."

"So it wasn't about us?"

Jamie did come to a stop then, turning his chair so he

faced her. "No, he did not ask about us. And so what if he did?"

Rachel shifted her weight and crossed her arms. "Well, I just would rather he didn't know you and I—" She broke off, not sure how to explain it to him without sounding insulting. "There's no need for him to know about us, okay?"

"So now we're a big secret?"

Rachel cringed at the scorn in his voice.

"No, of course not." She frowned. "That's not what I meant. I just don't see any need to tell people we're in a—a relationship, when both of us know it's only temporary."

Jamie snatched his sunglasses off. "I'm not going to lie if someone asks me about us," he said, his voice hard with disbelief. "If you're uncomfortable with that, then you're always free to just walk away." He inched closer, and Rachel found her breath catch at the intensity in his blue eyes. "Well?"

"Well, what?"

He slid his sunglasses back on and smiled. "You're not walking away, so I guess that means you're sticking around."

Rachel arched an eyebrow as he adroitly spun his chair around and made his way toward the van, but she couldn't quite suppress the smile that tugged at her mouth.

JAMIE SAT IN the back of the van and watched Rachel in the

rearview mirror, unwilling to admit how anxious he'd been when he'd all but given her an ultimatum. He'd half expected her to call his bluff and leave him there in the parking lot. Now he closed his eyes behind his sunglasses and tipped his head back against the seat, feeling relieved and guilty at the same time.

He'd lied to Rachel.

Dylan hadn't just asked if he was sleeping with Rachel; he'd all but accused Jamie of taking advantage of his sister while she was emotionally vulnerable. Jamie wasn't buying it, of course. Rachel's marriage had been over for a long time. Those divorce papers were no more than a formality. There was no question in his mind she was better off without the Deke-wad. Dylan had at least agreed with him on that point, but had disagreed Jamie was what Rachel needed. He'd had some valid points, but when he'd insisted the difference in their ages was a contributing factor, Jamie had refused to listen, and had left.

He and Rachel were pretty great together. Better than great—they were amazing. He had plans to return to California, too, so they were on the same page if she really intended to open her own business on the West Coast. She was smart and funny, and they never ran out of things to talk about.

And the sex was off-the-charts phenomenal.

Their age difference was the one thing he couldn't control, but he refused to let it be a deal-breaker. As far as he was concerned, Rachel was in the prime of her life. She was beautiful, in great shape, and she still had years in which to start a family, if that's what she wanted. Lots of women were waiting until their mid to late thirties to have babies. He especially liked that she was mature. She didn't play head games the way so many younger women did. He didn't want a girl; he wanted a woman.

He wanted Rachel.

He thought again of his conversation with Dylan, and tried to suppress his frustration. He told himself it didn't matter what other people thought. All he had to do was convince Rachel.

Chapter Thirteen

JAMIE PUT THE unpleasant conversation with Dylan out of his head, and focused instead on enjoying the time he had with Rachel. It had been years since he had watched a rodeo. Since the three-day event seemed to be all people at the lodge were talking about, they agreed it would be a fun way to pass a few hours, and made their way to the fairgrounds.

After parking the van, Rachel automatically reached for Jamie's wheelchair, and he saw her surprise when he stopped her.

"I can get by with my crutches," he said. "It will be easier."

Rachel frowned. "Are you sure? I don't want you to overtire yourself."

Jamie gave her a lecherous grin. "Don't worry, sweetheart; I'll be sure to save enough energy for tonight."

She gave a surprised laugh. "Jamie Colter, you're unbelievable."

As she leaned through the open door of the van to reach for his crutches, he took the opportunity to kiss her, gratified when she gave a small sigh and leaned in to him, kissing him back until finally they broke apart, breathless.

"We don't have to see the rodeo today," Jamie said, his voice husky with suggestion. "It'll still be here tomorrow."

Rachel leaned in and pressed her mouth against his. "As tempting as that sounds, I promised Dylan we'd come back later, so we only have a few hours." She pulled back and looked at him, before stroking her thumb across his mouth, her smile full of promise. "But I'll make it up to you tonight. Deal?"

Jamie gave a soft groan. "Lady, you are killing me."

But Rachel just laughed softly.

They made their way to the ticket booth at the edge of the fairgrounds, and Jamie could already hear the call of the announcer and cheers of the crowd. A carnival was underway on the far side of the fairgrounds, and he could see the giant Ferris wheel turning overhead, and smell the aromas of funnel cakes and fried foods.

Jamie paid for their tickets, and they found two seats on the lower tier of the grandstands that allowed Jamie ample room to extend his leg.

The stadium was nearly full, and Jamie breathed in the familiar smells of dust, leather, and fresh manure. He, Dylan, and Lucas had spent many days during their youth attending local rodeos, and Lucas had declared he was going to be a bull rider when he grew up. That had never happened, of course, since he lived on Long Island, and there seemed to be a shortage of cowboys in New York. Instead, he'd attended

West Point and had been commissioned into the Army following graduation. He'd gone through a series of grueling physical and mental tests and had been selected for the elite Special Forces. Jamie kept in touch with him, and knew he had recently been deployed to the Middle East. While he, Lucas, and Dylan didn't see as much of each other as they had when they were kids, Jamie liked to think their friendship was still as solid as it had always been.

"What is this event?" Rachel bumped his shoulder with her own, pulling him out of his thoughts.

He surveyed the arena, and saw an enormous steer snorting impatiently in the chute, and a cowboy on horseback waiting in the chutes on either side.

"This is the steer-wrestling," he said. "They'll release the steer, and that cowboy there will try to wrestle it to the ground. That other cowboy is called the *hazer*. He'll ride alongside the steer to make sure it runs straight."

Rachel looked at the steer, concern clouding her eyes. "Isn't that dangerous?"

Jamie nodded. "There's a lot of risk for the cowboy, if he doesn't get a good hold on the steer."

They watched as the cowboy nodded to the caller, and the steer was released, followed immediately by the hazer. The steer was big and layered with muscle, and Jamie thought the cowboy would have a tough time bringing it down. The cowboy exploded from his chute as soon as the restraining rope came free, and he thundered across the arena until he was parallel to the steer.

Rachel moved closer to Jamie and clutched his arm as the cowboy leaned over the side of his galloping horse and grabbed the horns of the running steer. She gasped as the cowboy was yanked off his horse by the rampaging steer, but he planted his booted heels into the dirt, dragging both himself and the massive animal to a slower pace.

They watched as the cowboy released the horns with one gloved hand and grabbed the animal's nose, pulling it off-balance and throwing it to the ground. The steer's legs went into the air, and the official waved a flag.

"That's it," Jamie said, as the cowboy released the steer and stood up, dusting himself off as he acknowledged the cheers of the crowd with a nod.

The steer, clearly indignant but no worse for the event, heaved himself to his feet and trotted off.

Rachel released her breath. "That was crazy!"

Jamie laughed. "Darlin', that was nothing. Wait until the bull riding starts!"

Rachel made a sound that was half-laugh, half-groan. "And here I thought I was just going to see some nice barrel racing, or maybe a bucking horse or two!"

They stayed long enough to watch the remainder of the steer-wrestling event, and then caught the beginning of the bull-riding competition. Jamie knew Rachel didn't enjoy that sport as much. She hid her face against his shoulder, certain the cowboy would be flung to his death, or gored by the bull.

After the third cowboy had completed his bull ride, Rachel declared she couldn't watch another cowboy risk his life.

"They're so young!" she exclaimed, as they made their way out of the grandstands. "How can their mothers even allow them to compete in something so dangerous?"

Jamie didn't want to tell her most of those cowboys were around his own age. That would only reinforce her belief he was too young for her. They made their way slowly through the fairgrounds to the midway, where Jamie bought them both a bratwurst sub, with some cold drinks. Rachel carried them to a table beneath a shady umbrella, and they ate in comfortable silence, watching the people go by.

"I bet this place is fun at night," Rachel commented, sipping her drink. "I haven't been to a country fair in years. I love all the bright lights and sounds."

"What, Times Square at night doesn't compare?" Jamie teased.

Rachel made a face at him. "Seriously, I miss these kinds of things."

"So what did you do for fun when you weren't working?"

Rachel thought for a moment. "Well, when I was still with Deke, we'd usually head out to one of his vacation houses, or maybe spend time on the family yacht." Seeing his expression, she frowned. "Don't judge. The guy has more money than you can even imagine, so his idea of recreation is a lot different than yours or mine. In his defense, that's the way he was raised, so that's all he knows."

"That guy has no defense," Jamie muttered. "Even if he wasn't filthy rich, he'd still be a dick."

Rachel gave him a half smile. "Probably."

"So now that you've returned to the real world, what do you enjoy doing in your free time?"

To Jamie's surprise, she leaned across the table and laced her fingers with his, as she gave him a shy smile. "Well, this is pretty nice. I like being back in Montana, and I like being with you."

Something shifted in Jamie's chest as she looked at him. He wanted to capture the moment and savor it. In the time since they'd been together, her eyes had never held the soft promise he saw reflected there now. Hope welled inside him. Could she be falling for him? Could he possibly mean more to her than just a temporary diversion?

He fervently hoped so.

"Hey, is that you, Colter?"

At the sound of the deep, surprised voice, Rachel snatched her hands away, pushing them down into her lap. Jamie shaded his eyes as he turned to see a couple with a child had stopped beside their table. He frowned, peering up at the man.

"Cole Tanner?"

The man's face broke into a grin, and he stepped forward to shake Jamie's hand. "I thought that was you. I heard you were home." He sobered, and gestured toward Jamie's leg.

"Hey, man, I was sorry to hear what you went through. Are you doing okay?"

Jamie nodded. "Yeah, thanks. I'll be getting this off in a few days. How've you been?"

Cole had grown up in Glacier Creek, and although he was a few years older than Jamie, they'd always been friendly.

"Things couldn't be better." Cole turned toward his companion, a slender, attractive woman with honey-brown hair and large, blue eyes. Holding her hand and staring at his cast with wide eyes was a little girl, no more than five or six, with corkscrew red hair and freckles. "Jamie, meet my fiancée, Joy Holliday, and her daughter, Piper."

Jamie shook both their hands, winking broadly at the little girl, who grinned at him and half-hid behind her mother. He gestured toward Rachel, who all but squirmed in her seat. "You remember Rachel McCafferty, right? She's Dylan's sister."

Cole's face registered surprise, which he quickly schooled into a friendly smile as he shook Rachel's hand. "Sure, I know Dylan. We jumped fires together before I left the forest service, and we built his house together a couple of years back. I haven't seen him yet this summer. How's he doing?"

Jamie briefly described Dylan's accident, and Cole was instantly sympathetic. "I'm sorry to hear that. I had no idea. Here I was wondering why the two of you would be together, but I get it now."

Jamie groaned inwardly as the other man all but solidified Rachel's fears about being seen with him.

"We're only in Bozeman until tomorrow," Cole continued, "but I'll stop by the hospital and see him, unless you think he's not up for visitors."

"I think he'd like to see you," Rachel said. "That would be really nice of you."

They talked for several more minutes, mostly about how Cole had recently taken over his family's timber-frame company, before they said their good-byes, promising to get together for a drink back in Glacier Creek.

"Well, that was awkward," Rachel commented, when Cole and Joy were out of earshot.

"How so?" Jamie asked, pretending to misunderstand. "Cole's a great guy, and he's a good friend of your brother's."

Rachel gave him a tolerant look. "He couldn't begin to fathom why you and I are together."

"Are we back to this again?" Jamie shoved his food away, no longer hungry. "I thought we had an agreement."

"I agreed we wouldn't talk about the difference in our ages, but that's not going to stop other people from talking and wondering." She gestured toward the passing crowd, where Cole and Joy could no longer be seen. "You must know this is how it's going to be every time someone sees us together."

Jamie leaned forward. "That's bull, and you know it. The only reason Cole even questioned it is because he knows—"

"—there's no reason why we would even be friends, never mind lovers," Rachel finished for him. "You know it's the truth."

"So let's do this," Jamie said, refusing to be drawn into an argument over something that seemed, at least to him, so trivial. "Let's bring it all out into the open, and let everyone know we're together. Glacier Creek isn't that big of a town, so if we tell a few people, I figure everyone's going to know inside of a week. They can get all their idle gossip and speculation out of the way, and within another week it will be old news. People will get used to seeing us together, and before you know it, nobody is going to care."

Rachel looked away. "I don't know…" She glanced at him. "Are we even going to be in Glacier Creek long enough for it to matter? Our parents will be back in less than a week." She groaned. "Actually, mine will probably be here tomorrow."

"In which case, we'll leave them to look after Dylan, and you and I can hightail it back to Glacier Creek. We have at least a week before my folks return, and your parents will probably stay here, until Dylan can be moved. We have some time to figure this out."

Rachel pressed her fingers against her temples. "Wait, wait. This is moving way too fast. Are you saying once our parents come home, we should tell them about us?"

Jamie forced himself to sound casual. "Sure. Why not?"

Rachel stared at him in disbelief. "Really? What about

your parents? Do you really think they'll be okay with us being together? Won't they think it's crazy?"

Honestly, Jamie didn't know how his parents would react. He didn't think his father would care, but his mother was a different story. She still thought of him as a kid, and couldn't help but fuss over him as much as he tried to discourage her.

He leaned forward and captured one of her hands in his. "I don't have all the answers, Rachel. All I know is our folks are coming home soon, and I'm not ready to end whatever this is between us. We're both adults, which means we get to make our own choices. So if you still want to be with me, we're going to have to go public, because I refuse to sneak around." He gave her a meaningful look. "We're both too old for that."

Rachel stared at him, and then nodded. "You're right. But can we at least have this next week to keep things under wraps? I promise once our parents and Dylan are back in Glacier Creek, if you still want to go public, then we will."

Jamie let out a slow, controlled exhalation of relief. He'd been half certain Rachel would take the coward's way out and end things now, before she was forced to face her family and friends. Hell, he'd end things if she felt that strongly about keeping their relationship a secret, as if it was something to be ashamed of. As if *he* was someone to be ashamed of.

He glanced at his watch. "It's just past one o'clock, and

I'm pretty beat. Why don't we go back to the lodge and, uh, take a nap?"

Rachel narrowed her eyes at him, but her mouth curved in a knowing smile. "Somehow, I don't think sleeping is what you have in mind."

"Nope," he agreed cheerfully.

If he stood even the smallest chance with Rachel, he needed to take every opportunity to remind her how good they were together.

Chapter Fourteen

THEY STAYED IN Bozeman for another two days, and when they weren't at the hospital with Dylan, they were either at the lodge making love, or exploring the area attractions. Rachel couldn't get enough of Jamie, and he seemed intent on holding her hand, or touching her in some other way when they were out in public. He was everything she had ever hoped for in a lover, alternately tender and possessive, showing her pleasure she had never dreamed possible.

He was inventive, and had no boundaries or inhibitions. Everything was a possibility with him, and although much of the sex was urgent and intense, he also made it fun and light-hearted. Rachel didn't think she'd ever laughed during sex before, the way she did with Jamie, just before he made her gasp and cry out in satisfaction.

Now, on their third day in Bozeman, they made their way through the corridors to Dylan's room. They had visited with him earlier that morning, and had returned to the lodge at noon. There, in the shadowed coolness of their room, Jamie had brought her to orgasm twice, before they'd showered and made love yet again on the wide bed, their bodies still slippery and wet.

Jamie refused to use his wheelchair, and now he easily swung beside her on his crutches. As they approached Dylan's room, they heard voices. She and Jamie exchanged a look.

"Here we go," he murmured.

They entered the hospital room to see Rachel's parents were there. Her mother sat by the bed and clutched Dylan's hand, while her father stood by the window and stared moodily out over the city toward the surrounding mountains. They both started when Rachel and Jamie entered the room, and Diane McCafferty rose to her feet to come around and give Rachel a hug.

"Thank you so much for coming down to be with your brother," she said. Pulling back, she searched Rachel's face. "Are you doing okay?"

Rachel nodded. "Of course, Mom."

Diane turned to Jamie, and cupping his face, gave him a motherly kiss on one cheek. "Thank you for coming with her, Jamie. I hope this hasn't been too hard on you."

"Not at all," Jamie assured her. "I've been exactly where Dylan is now, and I know how much I appreciated having visitors when I was confined to a hospital bed."

Dylan made a snorting sound, and they all looked at him.

"What?" he grumbled. "It's not like you even spend

much time here. I guess the local sights are more interesting than hanging out with me."

Rachel's face went warm, and she didn't dare look at Jamie. Dylan was right; aside from a quick visit each morning, and a longer one in the afternoon and evening, they hadn't exactly camped out in his room.

"You need your rest more than you need us disturbing you," she said quickly. "And Cole Tanner and his fiancée came to see you, so it's not like you haven't had plenty of company."

"So what have you been doing to stay busy?"

This from Rachel's father, John. Was it her imagination, or did she detect a note of suspicion in his tone?

"Sir, we've been taking in the rodeo, which is where we ran into Cole Tanner," Jamie said smoothly. "I haven't been to Bozeman in a long time, so I've enjoyed getting out and seeing the city, and Rachel has been nice enough to chauffeur me around."

"Ah, yes, the Bozeman Stampede Rodeo," her father mused. "I would have liked to see that myself. Been a long time since I've seen a rodeo." He nodded. "Well, glad to see you're feeling well enough to enjoy the sights."

"Thank you, sir," Jamie said.

"What are your plans now?" John asked. "Maybe we can have dinner together tonight. Where are you staying?"

"Dad, we're going to head back to Glacier Creek," Rachel interjected, before Jamie could speak. "Jamie has an appointment with the orthopedic surgeon tomorrow that he can't miss. Now that you and Mom are here, we can leave Dylan in your capable hands."

"Oh," Diane said in surprise. "I was hoping you might be able to stay for a few days."

"I'm sorry, Mom, but that won't be possible," Rachel said, infusing her voice with disappointment. "I'm sure you understand."

"Of course we do," her mother replied. "I'm just grateful you were able to get here so quickly after his accident."

Diane reached again for Dylan's hand, and her brother gave Rachel a look that told her clearly he wasn't fooled by her story. For the first time, she understood Jamie's reluctance to keep their relationship a secret. She didn't enjoy telling her family the fib about Jamie's doctor appointment. While he did have an appointment, it wasn't for three more days. She and Jamie could certainly stay in Bozeman, but she was anxious to have him all to herself, away from her family's curious eyes.

She and Jamie stayed and visited for another hour, listening to her parents enthuse about their abbreviated cruise, which led to Jamie and Dylan swapping stories from when they were growing up together, including when they had accompanied their parents on a cruise and had raised holy hell. Rachel didn't have a lot to add, since she had been in college during that time, and her focus hadn't been on the boys.

Finally, Rachel rose to her feet.

"Well, we should probably hit the road, since it'll take us four hours to get home," she said.

Jamie stood up, and Diane came around the end of the bed to hug them both. "Drive safely. We'll see you soon."

"Um, when do you think that might be?" Rachel asked, trying to sound casual.

"The doctor thinks he should be ready to travel in a week," her father said.

"Who's been feeding Boomer?" Rachel asked Dylan. Boomer was his enormous Maine coon cat.

"I asked my neighbor to do it."

Rachel nodded. "Okay. I'll make sure the house is stocked with groceries, and that you have everything you need when you get home."

Dylan raised his eyebrows. "You would do that for me?"

"Of course." She eyed him speculatively. "Do you want me to rent a hospital bed? Sometimes it's easier to get out of, with the tilt function."

"You sound like you know this from experience," he said drily, giving her a knowing look.

"Jamie doesn't use a hospital bed," she replied. The words were out of her mouth before she realized just how revealing they were.

"I should have had one brought to the house when I first came home," Jamie interjected quickly. "Having the ability to elevate the foot of the bed is a lot better than trying to stuff pillows under your leg."

Rachel pretended to fish in her pocketbook for her sunglasses, unable to meet anyone's eyes.

"We should get going," she mumbled. With a rushed good-bye, she turned and walked out of the room, leaving Jamie to follow her. They made their way to the hospital entrance in silence, until finally Rachel looked over at him. He gave her a meaningful grin.

"What?" she demanded.

"Nothing," he said, laughing. "But for someone who wants to keep us a secret, you just about told everyone in that room we're sleeping together."

"I did not."

She gave the glass doors a hard push and walked outside, not bothering to hold the door open for Jamie. She heard him give a surprised shout, just before he started laughing again.

THEY ARRIVED BACK in Glacier Creek at dusk, having been delayed by several hours due to a major accident on the highway ahead of them. Rachel pulled into her parents' driveway and killed the engine. She stretched her arms over the steering wheel, easing the tightness from her shoulders and back.

"Ooh, that was a long drive," she said. "I'm so tired, and

so hungry I could eat a horse."

Behind her, Jamie slid the door of the van open and climbed out, hitching his crutches beneath his arms. She watched him in the rearview mirror. For a guy with one leg in a cast, he was disgustingly nimble. She stepped out of the van and went around to the cargo trunk to retrieve their bags.

"I've got that," Jamie said, taking his duffel bag and throwing it over one shoulder. "Listen, why don't you come over and I'll cook us both some dinner? We can head over to Dylan's place in the morning."

Rachel pushed a hand through her hair, and smiled at him. "That sounds good, but right now I really want to take a shower."

"Come take one at my place."

She couldn't help but laugh at the lecherous look he gave her. "I don't have any clean clothes at your house."

"Who said you'll need clothes?"

"If I come over now," Rachel said, stepping closer to him and rubbing her fingers along the roughness of his jaw, "then the likelihood of you cooking me dinner is about nil, and I really am hungry." She pressed a soft kiss against his tempting mouth. "I promise you I'm much, much better company after I'm showered and fed."

Jamie gave a groan and deepened the kiss, slanting his mouth across hers and feasting on her lips until finally, she pulled away.

"You're dangerous." She pressed another, swift kiss against his mouth and turned away with a smile. "I'll see you shortly."

"How shortly?" he called after her.

"Fifteen minutes!"

"Don't make me come get you!"

Rachel laughed, and let herself into the dark house. She'd just grab a quick shower and some clean clothes, and be over at Jamie's house well before the allotted fifteen minutes were up. She would have been happy to take a shower at his house, but she would never make it past his bed. Even now, her body thrummed with anticipation of what the night would bring. After spending the last several nights in his arms, she didn't want to sleep alone tonight. She'd never felt this way about anyone before, not even Deke during the early days of their romance.

She made her way through the house to her bedroom, stripping off her clothes as she went. She turned on the shower and let the water grow warm as she pulled a clean change of clothing from her dresser and laid it on the bed. Closing the bathroom door, she stepped under the spray and quickly washed her hair and soaped her body, before running a razor over her legs and underarms. Jamie seemed mesmerized by her skin, always reflecting on how smooth and soft it was, so she didn't want to disappoint him.

She stepped out of the shower and swiftly wrapped a towel around her hair. There would be no time to blow it dry, but somehow she didn't think Jamie would care. She swiped the condensation from the mirror with the palm of her hand, and quickly brushed her teeth, checking the time on her watch. Twelve minutes had passed since she'd entered the house, which left her just three minutes to get dressed and get over to Jamie's house.

Pulling open the bedroom door, she stopped in her tracks. Jamie stood leaning on his crutches by the bed, idly fingering the lacy bra she had left there. He angled his head to look at her, and the heat simmering in his eyes was so potent that Rachel felt the moisture on her skin evaporate.

"What are you doing here?" she asked, stepping closer. "I still have three minutes."

"I couldn't wait."

Dropping the bra, he turned toward her. He'd changed his shirt, and Rachel saw his short hair was damp.

"You took a shower," she said, and closed the distance between them. Reaching out, she swiped a single bead of water from his neck with her fingertip. He smelled good, like spicy soap and shampoo. "Why do I have the feeling that we won't be having any dinner?"

Jamie searched her eyes, and a smile tugged at his mouth. "Maybe I can wait. Let me cook you something."

"Later," she breathed. "Right now, you're the only thing I'm hungry for." Leaning up, she kissed him. He made a low sound of approval in his throat, and Rachel could taste his need, his urgency. Yet when one hand came up to frame her jaw, his fingers were gentle.

Dragging her mouth from his, she slowly let her towel drop to the floor. Jamie's eyes darkened with desire as he looked at her, and Rachel felt her body respond. Her nipples tightened, and her inner muscles clenched. He let his hands trail down to cover her breasts, his thumbs skimming over the small, tight buds. Rachel drew in a sharp breath.

"I love your body," he said, almost reverently. His breathing had quickened. "You're so beautiful, so warm and soft. So feminine."

Rachel smiled. "You're making me blush."

Jamie looked bemused. "Why? You must know how gorgeous you are."

"Let's just say I haven't heard that in a very long time. At least," she amended, covering his hands with her own, "not until I met you."

Moving to sit on the edge of the bed, Rachel drew him forward to stand between her knees. Looking up at him, she smiled at his taut expression and reached for the waistband of his shorts. He was already hard beneath the cotton fabric, and when she curled her hand around his length, he let out a hissing sound of pleasure.

"Are you doing okay?" she asked.

"Oh, yeah," he said hoarsely.

Pushing the shorts down, Rachel leaned forward and took him in her mouth. Jamie groaned loudly and put a hand on her head, sifting his fingers through her damp hair.

"Damn, that feels good," he said, his voice rough. "But if you keep going like that, I'm not going to last."

Rachel released him and climbed onto the bed on her knees, pulling him forward until he set his crutches aside and eased himself onto the mattress, shucking his T-shirt, and kicking his sandals off. Rachel tugged his shorts off, loving how he watched her through half-closed eyes, his breathing a little ragged, as if she was the sexiest woman alive. With Jamie, she could almost believe she was.

"I want you inside me," she breathed, and crawled over his body, kissing her way along the length of his muscular legs, lingering briefly over his straining erection, before continuing a moist path across his stomach and over his heaving chest, until she finally captured his mouth in hers.

Jamie caught her face in his hands and kissed her deeply, licking inside her mouth and feasting on her lips like a starving man. When she reached between their bodies to take him in her hand, he made a rough sound of need. Then she was sliding over him, loving how he stretched and filled her. He slid his hands over her back until he cupped her rear end, squeezing and massaging her flesh before he began to move, thrusting deeply as she rocked against him.

Breaking the kiss, Rachel watched his face as she rode him, watched as pleasure caused his features to grow taut and his muscles to coil tightly. She knew he was close, could feel how he tried to hold back. When he looked into her eyes, the intensity of the emotions she saw reflected there nearly undid her.

"I don't want to come without you," he muttered, and shifted beneath her, angling his hips so that he maximized contact with the most sensitive part of her.

The sensation was almost too much, the friction her undoing. The pressure gathered and built, and then coalesced into a single, brilliant point of blinding pleasure. Jamie gave a deep groan, and as he found his release, pulsing strongly inside her, she contracted tightly around him as wave after wave crashed over her, until finally she collapsed against him.

Her face was buried in the crook of his neck, and beneath her palm his heart beat hard and fast. Reaching down, he snagged the corner of a quilt folded at the foot of the bed and dragged it over them both. Rachel moved to his side and flung an arm across his chest, and a leg over his hips. His shoulder cushioned her head as she smothered a yawn. The combination of the long drive from Bozeman, the hot shower and the even hotter sex, made Rachel feel suddenly drowsy. Beneath the quilt, their combined body heat made for a warm cocoon, and she snuggled closer to Jamie.

"Oh, this is nice," she murmured.

"You bet," he agreed, his voice warm and fuzzy with contentment. He was quiet for a long moment. "Did you mean what you said earlier? Deke never told you how gorgeous you are?"

Rachel shifted. She didn't want to talk about Deke. "Maybe in the beginning—I don't really remember."

He made a sound that said he didn't believe her, but thankfully didn't pursue the topic. But Rachel couldn't help recalling the awful things Deke had said to her, in front everyone who had been there that day. By the time Deke had finished disparaging her in every way possible, whatever had been left of Rachel's self-esteem had been completely destroyed.

But with Jamie, she felt her former confidence returning. He made her feel good about herself. He made her feel excited about her future. He made her laugh the way she hadn't in years. He made her feel young and vibrant again.

Beside her, Jamie's breathing had deepened, and she knew he was nearly asleep. Despite all the positive feelings he engendered in her, she couldn't help feeling panicky.

Things were out of control. Their relationship had gotten way too serious, way too intense, way too quickly. She'd lost her perspective. She no longer had the ability to think rationally where Jamie was concerned.

Was he too young? She wanted a family, but maybe he wasn't ready for that kind of commitment. She didn't even know if she was ready for that kind of commitment. A week ago, she'd just about sworn off men altogether.

How would their families feel if they announced they were a couple? Jamie was her younger brother's best friend, and she already knew Dylan disapproved. She'd endured the blatant disapproval of Deke's parents; she wasn't sure she could handle that from Jamie's parents.

He'd told her he wanted to rejoin his unit, but what did that mean? Would he deploy overseas again? Would they be separated by time and distance, the way she and Deke had been? What kind of relationship could work under those conditions?

The troubling thoughts tumbled through her head as she lay awake, staring at the ceiling and listening to Jamie's breathing. She didn't have the answers, but she knew she had to make some decisions soon, before she fell completely and hopelessly in love with the man.

She was afraid it might already be too late.

Chapter Fifteen

RACHEL ROSE EARLY and crept out to the kitchen, leaving Jamie to sleep.

In the kitchen, she went through the motions of making coffee, like an automaton. She felt wrung out, both physically and emotionally. She didn't think she'd slept more than a few hours all night, going back and forth in her head about all the reasons she and Jamie were wrong for each other.

And all the reasons they were right.

As the coffee dripped, she pictured him in the bedroom, sprawled on his back in bed, his gorgeous mouth slack in sleep, naked beneath the sheets. A wave of doubt washed over her. If she ended things, was she prepared never to see him like that again? Never hear his breath catch as she touched him intimately? Never watch his face tighten in pleasure, or hear the deep, appreciative sounds he made as she took him into her body?

Pouring herself a steaming mug of coffee, Rachel opened the sliding doors to the patio and stepped outside, breathing in the cool morning air. The yard was in shadow except for the patio table and chair, and Rachel sat down for a moment, enjoying the warmth of the sun on her face. The ring of the phone in her pocket startled her and she fished it out, knowing it would be Jamie. Did she dare answer?

Only it wasn't Jamie, it was her mother.

Drawing a deep breath, Rachel answered.

"Hi Mom, you're up early." She picked up her coffee mug and curled her fingers around its warmth.

"So are you," Diane replied. "I just wanted to check that you made it home safely."

"Yes, thanks. It was a long drive, but uneventful. How are you guys doing?"

"We're fine. We found a cute little B&B just outside the city, so we're trying to think of this as an extension of our original vacation."

"Hmm." Rachel sipped her coffee. "A bit different than a Hawaiian cruise."

"It certainly is, but I can't imagine being anywhere but right here, with your brother." She paused. "How is Jamie doing?"

"He's fine," she answered cautiously. "Why?"

"So he's not there with you?"

The question was so unexpected that Rachel blurted out a denial before she had time to really consider her words.

"No! Jamie is not here with me," she said, indignant. "It's barely seven o'clock. Why would you even ask that?"

"I don't know," her mother mused thoughtfully. "I got the sense there might be something between the two of you.

Dylan certainly seemed to think so."

"Well, Dylan is an idiot, and he's on some serious painkillers, so I wouldn't take anything he says as truth," she retorted. She didn't know why she couldn't tell her mother the truth. If there had ever been a time to come clean about her relationship with Jamie, this was it, but Rachel found she couldn't do it. She wasn't ready. Not yet.

"So you're not...dating?" her mother pressed.

"No! Jeez, Mom!" Rachel exclaimed. "Jamie Colter and I are definitely not dating!" She squeezed her eyes shut, hating the lies coming out of her mouth. "First of all, he's way too young for me, and secondly, he's probably no better than my ex, too impressed with himself to make a good partner."

A sound behind her startled her, and she turned in her chair to see Jamie standing in the open door to the house. Now he stared at her with an expression of stunned disbelief.

Rachel's mouth went dry, and her heart plummeted to her stomach.

"Mom, I have to go," she said, and disconnected the call.

She stood up, but Jamie was already turning away. "Jamie, wait! Let me explain!"

Jamie spun around on his crutches, and Rachel's throat constricted. His face was pale, and twin patches of color rode high on his cheekbones. His blue eyes blazed with anger, and something else. Disappointment? Regret?

"Don't bother explaining," he bit out. "I get it."

"Jamie, please let me explain—"

"Don't bother. You already said it all, and when you begin comparing me to Deke Narducci, then there's nothing left to say." He started to turn away, and then spun back, his face tight with suppressed emotion. "But you know what? You're right about one thing—the age difference is never going to work for us. You keep harping on how you're too old for me, but you're the one who's acting like a teenager.

"I need a woman, Rachel. I want a partner, equal in every way, not someone who can't make up her mind, who's more worried about what people will think, who doesn't know a good thing when it's staring her right in the face, and who doesn't appreciate something like this only comes around once in a lifetime—if you're lucky. So call me when you grow up."

Rachel reached for his arm, intent on stopping him, but he threw her off with one angry motion and kept going. She listened as the front door slammed shut, knowing she'd just made a terrible mistake.

JAMIE COULDN'T REMAIN in his parents' house, not with Rachel living across the street. He went hour to hour, alternately despising her and then despising himself.

He didn't want to see her.

He didn't know if he could go one more minute without seeing her.

He kept replaying the conversation he'd overheard, over and over again in his head. She couldn't have said anything more insulting if she'd tried, especially considering what they'd shared just the night before. He'd actually convinced himself that she was falling in love with him; that they had a chance of making a go of a real relationship. He was such an idiot.

He could maybe have forgiven her for lying to her mother about the fact they were sleeping together, and even the comment about him being too young for her. But he didn't think he could forgive her for comparing him with Deke Narducci.

He felt all torn up inside, and for the first time in his life, he didn't have a plan. All he could think was that he'd blown it. He'd had two weeks to prove he was perfect for her, and he'd blown it. He couldn't stay. If he did see her, or if she decided to come over, he'd lose it. He'd tell her he loved her, and beg her to stay, and that's not what she needed.

No, he'd meant what he'd said when he'd told her he wanted a partner, a woman who would see him as an equal and be proud to be seen with him. Until that happened, they could never have anything.

He didn't want to leave, but for his own sanity, he had to.

He quickly made a phone call to Dylan at the hospital in Bozeman. Then he packed a duffel bag. He needed to leave before Rachel decided to check in on him as part of her concierge services. Her conscience wouldn't allow her to just turn her back on him, but no way did he want her pity. He could take care of himself.

Twenty minutes later, he was stretched out on the back seat of Cole's SUV. Thankfully, the other man didn't ask any questions, and kept the conversation carefully neutral. They made a couple of stops, at Frank's supermarket and the liquor store, before they arrived at their destination. Jamie eased himself out of the truck, and swung his duffel bag over his shoulder, while Cole hefted the groceries and beer.

"Dylan said the key would be under the mat," Cole said, juggling the case of beer as he bent down and retrieved the key. "Laurel—she's the neighbor who's been feeding Boomer—said to call her if you have any questions about anything."

Jamie waited as Cole unlocked the door and stepped inside. He set the bags onto an island, and Jamie dropped his duffel bag inside the door. An enormous, gray and black cat with long hair and a bushy tail, wandered lazily into the kitchen and sat down by the island, where he blinked at the two men.

"You must be Boomer," Jamie said, and leaned down to scratch the cat behind the ears. "Looks like we're going to be housemates."

This was the first time he'd seen Dylan's house. Straightening, he moved over to the sliding doors on the far side of the kitchen. The log home had been built on the side of a mountain, and from the wide deck he could see Flathead Lake below, and the distant Mission Mountains.

"What a sweet view," he admired. He could even see part of downtown Glacier Creek, including the spire of the church, and the dock that extended out over the water.

"Want a beer?" Cole asked, and without waiting for a response, cracked two bottles and joined Jamie on the deck. "I helped Dylan build this house."

"Is this one of your house plans?" Jamie asked in surprise.

Cole grinned. "Yep. Dylan wanted something small to start, but the floor plan allows for expansion, should he ever decide to settle down and have a family."

Jamie laughed. "Somehow, I don't see that happening anytime soon. Dylan likes his bachelor lifestyle."

"That's only because he hasn't met the right woman."

Jamie took a long swallow of beer and angled his head to look at the other man. "Yeah, it's pretty powerful stuff, when it does happen."

"Damn right."

"So when's the wedding?"

"A couple of months," Cole said. "Joy wanted to wait for the foliage to turn. We're getting married out by the lake, at the Snapdragon Inn. I'll make sure you get an invite."

"Yeah, I'd like that," Jamie said, and he meant it. Too many years had passed since he'd reconnected with his friends in Glacier Creek. It would be good to see everyone.

They sat in companionable silence, enjoying the cold

beers and the majestic views, until Cole finally stood up.

"Well, I should probably get going."

Setting his beer aside, Jamie stood up and shook Cole's hand. "Thanks, man," he said. "I really appreciate the help."

"Anytime." Cole rubbed a hand over the back of his head and squinted at Jamie. "You can tell me to butt out, but does your moving out here have anything to do with Rachel McCafferty?"

Jamie gave a snort. "How'd you guess?"

"Your hangdog attitude was my first clue," Cole joked. "But seriously, I didn't realize you two were together when I saw you in Bozeman. I mean, I know you were together, but I thought it was only to visit Dylan. But Joy said the two of you are an item. Is she right?"

Jamie blew out a hard breath. "We were, yeah. Was it that obvious?"

Cole laughed. "Not to me, but I can be pretty obtuse. But Joy said she could tell just from the way Rachel looked at you."

"And how's that?"

"Joy said she had the look of a woman in love."

Jamie sharpened his gaze on Cole. "She said that?"

"Yup."

"Well, I wish that was true, but she's having second thoughts." He sighed deeply. "Maybe I'm the fool for thinking I could actually make her love me. Maybe I'm chasing a fantasy—something that never existed except in my own imagination."

Cole's expression was sympathetic. "If she's as smart as I think she is, she'll come around."

Jamie nodded. "I hope you're right."

Cole reached out and gave him a friendly slap on the shoulder. "Good luck. I'll come back the day after tomorrow and give you a lift to the doctor's office."

"Thanks. I appreciate that."

Cole pulled his phone out of his back pocket and scrolled through his list of contacts. "I'm going to leave you Laurel Cavanaugh's number, just in case. She lives just down the road. She's a writer and she works from home, so she's usually around. If you get stuck, give her a call, okay?"

"Thanks." Jamie watched as he wrote the number on a slip of paper and left it on the island.

They returned to the front porch, and Jamie watched Cole drive away. He turned and went back into the house, where Boomer stretched and yawned hugely, before rubbing his head against Jamie's cast.

He snagged another beer and made his way back out to the deck, where he lowered himself into a wooden Adirondack chair. Dylan's house was great, the view was fantastic, and he would soon be getting the cast on his leg removed, which would enable him to be independent once more. He could start making plans to return to his unit in California, which was what he wanted, right? So why did life look so freaking bleak?

Chapter Sixteen

THREE DAYS HAD passed since Jamie had left the house on Pinewood Avenue. Rachel had no idea where he'd gone, only that he was gone. It had only taken her a few hours after their ugly confrontation to realize the magnitude of the mistake she'd made. She'd run across the street, ready to tell Jamie what an idiot she'd been, but the house had been locked up tight. She'd gone around to the back and peered through the French doors into the kitchen, but her heart already knew the house was empty.

He had left without so much as a good-bye. Without allowing her an opportunity to make amends. The expression in his eyes just before he'd left still haunted her. She'd hurt him, and deeply. She'd expected him to be angry, but she hadn't expected him to leave. She hadn't seen or heard anyone pull up to the house, and had no idea where he might have gone. For all she knew, he could be on a flight back to Oceanside, California, where he had a condo.

With Dylan and her parents still in Bozeman, she'd never been lonelier. Only pride kept her from calling her brother at the hospital to see if he had any idea where Jamie might have gone. She'd called Jamie's cell phone numerous times, but each time it had gone to voicemail. Rachel didn't know if he had his phone turned off, or if he just didn't want to talk to her.

Finally, tired of feeling sorry for herself, she'd gone into town to listlessly poke through the shops, and had even walked out onto the pier, crowded with tourists and young families. But that only reminded her of when she'd visited the pier with Jamie, and how he'd brashly declared to anyone and everyone that she was the most beautiful girl in Glacier Creek.

For the first time since she'd headed off to college and New York City, she regretted that she hadn't maintained any of her friendships in Glacier Creek. Life had moved too fast, sweeping her along with it until one day she looked up and realized fifteen years had passed. In all those years, she'd only contacted her high-school friends once or twice, when she'd been home for a holiday or other family event. She hadn't attended any of her class reunions, or tried to maintain her old friendships, mostly because Deke had never wanted to spend any time with her family or her friends.

Instead, she'd had a few superficial friendships with the socialites who hung out on Deke's yacht, or temporarily lived at one of his many residences. When Rachel had questioned Deke about it, he'd always brushed her concerns aside, saying those same people would be more than willing to open their doors to him and Rachel in return.

Only they never had, at least when she'd accompanied Deke.

In retrospect, they had not been true friends. They had only wanted to hang out with Deke because he provided anything and everything they needed, at no charge, including booze and drugs.

She thought of her mother and Mrs. Colter, who had been friends since before Rachel was born. They'd weathered good times and bad times, yet their friendship had never wavered. Similarly, Jamie had managed to stay connected with Dylan and Cole and most of the other guys he'd hung out with as a kid. He hadn't ditched them just because he'd joined the Marines and had deployed halfway around the world.

That's what she wanted.

Something real.

Something permanent.

Now she sat on the town pier and looked out over the lake, where the windblown white caps ruffled the water, and gulls floated lazily on the air currents. Nearby, a little boy cried out in delight as he and his father caught a small fish, and reeled it in. Rachel watched as the father showed the boy how to carefully remove the hook, and then return the fish to the water where it could grow bigger.

Rachel closed her eyes and tipped her face up to the sun, listening to the sounds of people laughing, the water lapping at the pilings beneath her, and the gulls crying overhead.

Suddenly, the thought of relocating to another large city held no appeal.

She realized she had no desire to go to California to start her own business.

She liked the feel of Glacier Creek, with its abundance of natural beauty, and its slower pace. She even liked how everyone in the small town seemed to know each other, as demonstrated by the many happy conversations she saw struck up on the sidewalks and in the shops. Sure, there were tourists, but even they seemed to be the kind who returned year after year, as they chatted with the shopkeepers and locals about what had changed since they'd last visited.

The alarm on her phone rang and she jerked upright, digging through her pocketbook until she found it, and turned it off. Shading the device with her hand, she peered at the display and realized today was Jamie's appointment to have his cast removed at the VA hospital in Kalispell. She had no idea if he was even still in the area, but this might be her only opportunity to see him, if he did keep the appointment. If she left right now, she might just catch him.

She made her way quickly back to the parking lot, determined to be at the hospital early. If Jamie did show up, nothing would prevent her from talking to him, and telling him how she felt. She'd made a mistake the other day, but she finally knew what she wanted and where she belonged, and that was with him.

If he would still have her.

With her heart thudding hard in her chest, she drove the van to the Kalispell veterans' hospital and parked beneath some shady trees, with a clear view of the entrance. The hospital was small, and the only other entrance was for the emergency room. If Jamie kept his appointment, this was the entrance he would use. Blowing out a hard breath, she put the windows down to take advantage of the breeze, and fixed her eyes on the entry.

More than an hour later, she decided he must have left Glacier Creek and canceled his appointment, when he suddenly walked through the front doors of the hospital. His cast was gone, and in its place he wore a knee-high boot made of plastic and foam. He still used crutches, and he had his head down as he made his way through the entry, before turning toward the far side of the parking lot.

Rachel devoured the sight of him, noting every small detail of his appearance. Quickly, she climbed out of the van and was just about to cross the distance between them, when someone called his name.

Jamie stopped, and so did Rachel. She watched as a woman came out of the hospital behind Jamie, hurrying to catch up with him. She was young, probably no older than Jamie. She had a fabulous figure and thick auburn hair pulled back in a messy bun. She wore a pair of black-rimmed glasses, but instead of making her look bookish, they only served to give her a sexy-librarian look.

Rachel frowned. She was too far away to hear what the

woman was saying, but clearly they knew each other. Did the woman work at the hospital? Was she a friend?

She waited, half expecting the woman to turn and go back inside, but instead she remained on the sidewalk, talking earnestly to Jamie as he listened and nodded. Then, as Rachel watched, she reached out and cupped Jamie's face, dipping her head to look into his eyes as she talked. It seemed to Rachel she was pleading with him. Then, almost convulsively, Jamie pulled her into his arms and hugged her hard as he buried his face in the curve of her shoulder, unheeding of the crutches that fell to the ground.

Too shocked to do anything more than stare, Rachel stood rooted beside the van, feeling her heart drop into her stomach. After a moment, the two broke apart and the woman bent to retrieve his crutches. She said something that made Jamie laugh, and hot jealousy consumed Rachel.

She watched as they turned and made their way across the parking lot. The woman kept one hand on Jamie's back, and even from where she stood, Rachel could see her rubbing between his shoulder blades, until finally they both climbed into a vehicle and were gone.

Rachel sagged against the van, stunned.

Who the hell was the other woman? Was she involved with Jamie? Was Jamie staying with her? Was she from Glacier Creek?

It occurred to Rachel that if she had been thinking straight, she might have been able to follow their car and discover where Jamie was staying. In the next instant, she felt a little sick to her stomach. Whatever she might be, she was not a stalker. She'd lost everything, but she still had her pride. If Jamie had already moved on, then she'd misread him—he wasn't ready for a serious commitment.

She climbed back into the van and sat there for a long time, staring with unseeing eyes at the parking lot. She couldn't quite grasp Jamie was still in Glacier Creek, or that she'd seen him with another woman. Just three days ago she'd been ready to give him up, convinced they weren't right for each other, and yet seeing him with that woman made her realize he was the only man she wanted.

She loved him.

They were all wrong for each other, but nothing felt as right as Jamie's arms around her.

They belonged together.

Rachel gripped the steering wheel, and then bent her head down onto her hands, willing herself not to cry. She had no one to blame but herself. She was the only one who could make things right with Jamie.

She straightened and dragged in several long breaths, willing herself to be strong. She didn't know how she was going to fix the colossal mess she'd made of her life, but she was going to try.

First, she needed to make some changes.

NOTHING HAD EVER felt as good as getting that damned cast removed, Jamie thought, as he gently worked the stiffness out of his leg. Well, except having Rachel in his arms. There wasn't anything that could compete with that.

She'd tried to call him numerous times over the past week, but he'd stubbornly refused to answer. If he did, he'd cave. He was total mush in her hands and there was no way he wanted her to know that. Right now, his pride was all he had left. He couldn't risk seeing her until he was sure he could keep his emotions in check.

He missed her.

More than that, he missed them, together. He'd been on the verge of calling her so many times, but then he'd remember the scorn in her voice as she'd compared him to the Deke-wad, and he'd set the phone aside.

Someone knocked on the door, and he called out a greeting, allowing himself to relax back on the sofa. The door opened, and Laurel Cavanaugh came into the living room. Tall and slender, with reddish hair and glasses she continually pushed up with one finger, she was Dylan's closest neighbor. He thought she might be pretty if only she'd smile more. He had a tough time reconciling the fact she was the bestselling author of a popular murder mystery series. Shy by nature, she preferred to be at her house writing her books, but Cole had asked if she could look in on Jamie, and she'd taken the request very seriously.

She wasn't at all his type, but Jamie liked her quiet, unassuming manner, and the fact she didn't ask him questions. When Cole had been unable to give him a ride to the hospital for his doctor appointment, Laurel had volunteered. He was grateful for her calming presence, especially when the doctor told him he would walk with a pronounced limp for the rest of his life, and that his combat days were likely over.

He still had a tough time processing that information. If he couldn't deploy with his unit, he wasn't sure he wanted to remain in the military. He wasn't cut out for a desk job or an administrative detail.

He'd left the hospital feeling as if his entire world had tilted sideways. Laurel had been the one to tell him the only restrictions he had were the ones he imposed on himself, and he could still do whatever he put his mind to. He hadn't wanted to hear that, but she'd planted the seed and over the past few days, he'd found himself reluctantly thinking about other options: ones that would keep him here in Glacier Creek.

"Hey," Laurel called in greeting from the kitchen. "I was at the farmer's market this morning, so I picked up some fresh corn and tomatoes, and a half dozen steaks." She leaned back to look at him through the doorway. "Dylan is coming home today, right?"

"Yeah, he should be here in an hour or so. Why did you get so many steaks?"

"His parents are going to be dropping him off, so I thought they might like to stay and have supper with him."

"You didn't have to do that, but thanks. Let me give you some money."

She waved his words away. "Absolutely not. That's what friends do for each other, right? Think of it as my way of welcoming Dylan home again."

"You're going to join us, I hope."

"Of course!" Laurel gave him an owlish look from behind her glasses. "I never pass up an opportunity to give Dylan a hard time."

"I'm sure he'll appreciate it," Jamie said drily.

She'd been taking care of Boomer—and himself—since he'd come to stay at the timber-frame house. Dylan had hinted there was more to Laurel than most people were aware, but he didn't elaborate. Jamie was pretty sure Laurel had a crush on Dylan, but didn't think her feelings were reciprocated. She wasn't Dylan's type. Although, to be fair, Dylan didn't seem to have a type.

"How's the leg today?" she asked.

Jamie shrugged. "About the same. No worse, so that's good."

He'd been working hard to regain his lost muscle strength, and had been practicing walking without his crutches. Even with the rigid boot, his leg was still too weak to completely support his weight, although he could now get by with just one crutch. A physical therapist came to the house twice a week and put him through his paces, and he hoped he would be able to walk without the remaining crutch by the end of the month.

"Did you talk with Dylan today?" Laurel asked.

"I did, this morning." He laughed softly. "If possible, he's feeling even more ornery than I am. With two cranky cripples in the house, you might want to do yourself a favor and avoid coming over."

Through the kitchen doorway, he watched Laurel set a dish of food onto the floor for Boomer, and then she came into the living room and surveyed him, surrounded as he was by Dylan's workout equipment.

"Neither of you scare me," she said, smiling. "Trust me when I tell you I've handled worse. And you're not going to heal faster by overtaxing your leg. Just so you know."

Jamie grunted. He didn't want to admit Laurel was right. He just wanted to be back on his feet. He'd be better equipped to face Rachel if he wasn't on crutches or stuck in a wheelchair. And he would face her—there had never been any doubt in his mind about that. He just needed to be able to catch her if she decided to run.

"What time did Dylan say he'd be here?" Laurel asked, pulling him out of his thoughts.

"About an hour."

"Okay, that sounds perfect. I'm going to head home now, but I'll be back when he gets here, okay? The steaks and beer are in the fridge, and I put the corn into some water to soak; I thought they'd be good roasted on the grill."

Jamie raised a hand in farewell as she let herself out, and

then rose to his feet and made his way outside to the deck. He leaned on the railing and surveyed the town of Glacier Creek, below, a hard knot of misery in his chest.

What was Rachel doing right now? Did she think of him? Did she miss him? Dylan had promised not to tell her where he was, but Jamie wondered how long it would be before she figured it out. He was actually surprised—and more than a little disappointed—she hadn't already discovered he was staying at Dylan's house. He'd have thought she'd be over long before now to make sure the house was ready for Dylan when he returned from Bozeman. The sun beat warm on his shoulders, reminding him there was cold beer in the fridge.

Turning, he made his way back into the house, and then stopped when he heard a key in the front lock. He paused, expecting Dylan or his parents to walk through the door.

The last person he expected to see was Rachel, and judging by the shocked look on her face when she saw him standing there, she hadn't expected to see him, either.

Chapter Seventeen

"WHAT ARE YOU doing here?"

They both said the words at the same time, and Rachel flushed. Jamie thought she looked pale, and there were dark smudges beneath her eyes, as if she hadn't slept well. Guilt gnawed at him, even as he devoured her with his eyes.

"I, um, promised to bring some groceries over," she explained.

For the first time, Jamie noticed she carried two grocery totes that bulged with food.

"Here, I'll take those," he said, and his voice sounded gruff, even to his own ears. He stepped forward and took both totes in one hand, and then turned to limp his way into the kitchen.

After a moment, he heard Rachel follow him.

"Believe me, I didn't plan this. I had no idea you would be here," she finally said, as he set the bags onto the island.

"Or you wouldn't have come?" Jamie sounded bitter, but he couldn't help himself. When he angled his head to look at her, his chest constricted. Rachel stood uncertainly just inside the kitchen, turning her car keys over and over in her hands and not looking at him.

"I'm not the one avoiding contact," she said quietly, and raised her gaze to his. "You haven't returned any of my calls."

"No."

A sudden knock on the door startled them both, and then the front door opened and Laurel poked her head inside. "Hello! It's just me! I saw a van pull up."

"We're in the kitchen," Jamie called.

Laurel came in, a wide smile on her face, and then came to an abrupt stop when she saw Rachel.

"Oh, I'm so sorry," she said, putting a hand to her throat. "I thought it might be Dylan. I didn't mean to intrude."

"Laurel, I'd like you to meet Dylan's sister, Rachel." Jamie nodded in her direction. "Rachel, this is Laurel Cavanaugh."

Laurel's face cleared, and she stepped forward with a wide smile. "Oh, what a pleasure it is to finally meet you! I've heard so much about you from Dylan!"

To Jamie's astonishment, Rachel didn't seem inclined to return Laurel's friendly smile. She shook the other woman's hand, but the overture seemed grudging, at best.

"So Jamie hasn't mentioned me?" Rachel asked, tipping her chin up and sliding a quick look at Jamie.

Laurel gave a small laugh, and looked confused. "No.

Why, should he have?"

"Rachel—" Jamie tried to interject, but Rachel held her hand up, forestalling whatever words he might have said.

"No, there's no reason why he should have mentioned me," she replied, but the smile she gave Laurel didn't reach her eyes. "And now that I've met you, I understand why."

"I, uh, think there's been some misunderstanding," Laurel said, casting a worried look toward Jamie. "Maybe I should go."

"I'll call you later," Jamie said.

He didn't know what had gotten into Rachel, but he didn't want her taking it out on Laurel, who had done nothing to deserve it. He waited until Laurel had closed the front door behind her, and then spread his hands out.

"What are you doing?"

To his astonishment, Rachel put a hand to her eyes and half turned away.

"I don't know," she muttered. "I wasn't expecting to see you here, and it just sort of threw me. I mean, I know you're with her now, but I didn't expect to actually see you with her, okay? I had no idea she would be here."

Jamie frowned. "Who? Laurel?"

"Yes, Laurel!" Rachel's voice broke. "I tried to call you, Jamie. It took me about an hour to figure out I'd made a mistake in letting you leave that day." She looked at him, stricken. "A huge mistake! I went over to your house, but you'd already left."

Jamie took a step toward her. "I couldn't stay, Rachel. You know that. Seeing you every day, being that close and not being able to be with you—I had to leave."

"And Laurel was right there to console you," Rachel said bitterly.

Jamie stared at her, dumbfounded. "What?"

Rachel turned to him, her face contorted in pain. "I saw you! I saw you together, Jamie, so don't try to deny it!"

Now Jamie did step forward, unmindful of his stiff leg, and took her by the shoulders. "I do deny it! What did you see, Rachel?"

She struggled not to cry and it was as if someone had ripped his beating heart from his chest. He dragged her into his arms, ignoring her stiff resistance, intent only on trying to soothe her.

"I saw you outside the hospital," she said, her voice muffled against his chest. "You were hugging her, and it looked like more than just a neighborly hug, and I almost don't blame you because she's beautiful and young—"

Jamie tightened his hold on her. "Oh, Rachel…"

JAMIE'S CHEST HEAVED up and down, and for just an instant, Rachel thought he might actually be crying, but when she lifted her face from his shoulder, she realized she was mistaken.

He was *laughing*.

Rachel leaned back in his arms and stared at him, even as a part of her brain registered he wasn't releasing her, and in fact seemed to be holding her even closer.

And it felt wonderful.

"What's so funny?" she demanded, and swiped her fingertips across her eyes.

"Laurel is nothing more than a friend," he said. His eyes traveled over her face like a caress. "That day at the hospital, the doctor gave me news I wasn't ready to hear, and she was just trying to make me feel better."

Hope flared inside of Rachel. Friends, not lovers!

"So you're not together?"

"Not even close. My heart already belongs to someone else."

"Oh, Jamie…" She started to melt against him, and then the full meaning of his words sank in. "What news did the doctor give you?"

"My leg will never be as strong as it was, and I'll always walk with a limp."

Rachel understood what it was he wasn't saying. "What does that mean for you? For your military career?"

"I'm not sure. I haven't been on active duty in almost six months, and I'm still facing months of rehab. If I can't return within a year, I'll be medically discharged."

Rachel tentatively raised a hand and laid it against his lean cheek. "If that means you won't deploy again, and you won't have bombs dropped on you while you're sleeping, then I can't be sorry."

His voice was cautious. "You sound as if you care."

Rachel's heart rate accelerated. She thought her display of jealousy might have been a clue as to how she felt, but now she realized he wasn't going to let her off that easily. If she really wanted to be with him, she was going to have to let him know in no uncertain terms.

She stroked the pad of her thumb over his lower lip, and then leaned up and pressed a soft kiss against his mouth.

"We belong together," she murmured against his lips. "You've given me the courage to finally stand up for myself and admit what it is I want, and I want you. You're the bravest, strongest, most decent man I know. I can't imagine being with anyone else."

Jamie gave a soft grunt, and although he lifted a hand to frame her jaw with his fingers, he didn't kiss her back. "You're going to have to show me," he breathed against her mouth. "I've been out of my mind this past week, thinking about you. You've put me through hell, so if you really want me, you need to show me."

"My parents and Dylan will be here soon," she reminded him.

"Then you'd better hurry."

Rachel smiled.

Sliding her arms around his neck, she slanted her mouth over his, reveling in the feel and taste of him. She'd missed this. She'd missed him. And when he gave a groan of surrender and slid his hand to the back of her head, opening his mouth to the sensuous slide of her tongue, she knew she'd won.

The kiss was urgent and hot, and when Jamie cupped her rear and pulled her against his hips, she was left in no doubt he wanted her.

"Not here," she managed to gasp. "Anyone could walk in on us."

"I don't care," he muttered. "I need to be inside you."

"The bedroom," she urged.

Jamie pulled away, and then grabbed his crutch, shoving it under his arm as he took her hand. "This way."

Rachel followed him through the living room to a short hallway that opened to a guest bedroom and a bathroom.

"In here." Jamie pulled her into the room, before closing and locking the door. "Come here," he said roughly, and hauled Rachel against his chest.

"I've missed you," she whispered, just before his mouth claimed hers in a kiss so searing, Rachel actually moaned.

Her hands worked their way beneath the hem of his T-shirt, stroking over the hard, smooth warmth of his stomach and chest. Jamie broke the kiss just long enough to drag the shirt over his head, and then he was completely bare-chested beneath her questing fingers.

Rachel swiftly worked the button on his cargo shorts, and slid the zipper down.

“Take these off,” she urged, and pushed them downward.

Jamie helped her, hooking his thumbs into the waistband of both his boxers and the shorts, and shoving them down to his knees, where he tried to kick them free.

“Here, let me,” Rachel said, and bent to work the clothing over the rigid boot. Without the full cast, she could now see the evidence of the injuries he’d sustained during the building collapse, and his leg was a mass of scars. Her heart swelled with love and anguish for what he’d endured, but also with pride for his courage. She pressed a soft kiss against the angriest of the marks, and then tipped her head back to look up at Jamie. Only that brought her eye-level with his gorgeous, impressive erection, which strained upward.

She couldn’t help herself; he was impossible to resist.

Curling her hand around the thick base, she ran her tongue over him, from bottom to top. He throbbed hotly in her hand, and she drew him into her mouth, smiling as she heard him gasp. He tasted delicious, and she swirled her tongue slickly around the crest, before sucking deeply on him. He groaned loudly, and plunged his fingers into her hair, massaging her scalp as she moved her mouth over him. Reaching beneath his shaft, she cupped him in her hand, teasing him gently as she sucked him harder, deeper. The sounds of pleasure he made caused desire to jack-knife through her, and a warm gush of moisture at her core made her squirm with need.

"Enough," he said, his voice a harsh rasp. "Or I'm not going to last."

Rachel released him, and with a last swipe of her tongue over the glistening head, she rose to her feet.

"Your turn," Jamie said, and drew her shirt over her head, and then reached behind her to unfasten her bra. Rachel let it drop to the floor, and closed her eyes as Jamie bent and took one nipple into his mouth, grazing the hard nub with his teeth, before sucking on it. She clutched at his shoulders, certain she would fall if not for his solid strength. With his free hand, he loosened the drawstring on her linen pants, and immediately pushed his other hand inside to stroke her intimately.

"Oh, God," he groaned, "you are so wet."

The touch of his fingers against the most sensitive part of her was almost her undoing, and she nearly came apart right then and there.

"Jamie," she gasped, and he lifted his head from her breast.

"I can't wait," he growled, and turned her so she lay across the bed. He bent and swiftly jerked her shoes and pants off, until she was completely naked.

He came over her, pushing her knees wide, and braced himself on one elbow. Rachel realized they had never made love with him on top, because of his leg. Now he rose over her, and she admired how the muscles in his shoulders and arms bunched and flexed with each movement. He took himself in his hand, and fitted the broad tip against her opening.

"We belong together," he said, searching her eyes. "Say it."

Rachel tried to push her hips upward, desperately seeking relief, but he easily held himself away.

"Say it," he insisted.

"Jamie…"

He gave her a meaningful look, and then deliberately stroked himself. His breathing quickened. If she didn't tell him what he needed to hear, he would bring himself to climax and deny her that pleasure.

"We belong together!" she said quickly, her eyes fixed on where his fist curled around his thick length.

"Do you mean it?" he asked.

Rachel raised her gaze to his, and searched his eyes. There was so much love there, but also wariness. He half expected her to disappoint him again.

"We belong together," she said softly. "You're everything I've ever hoped for in a partner, and we belong together."

Jamie closed his eyes briefly, and then fitted himself against her and surged forward, stretching and filling her until she cried out with the sheer pleasure of it. She was so aroused, it would take no more than a few strokes to push her over the edge.

Fully seated inside her, Jamie paused with his head pressed against her neck, not moving. Rachel groaned and lifted her hips, seeking the friction she needed.

"Don't move," Jamie commanded.

He raised his head to look at her, and she saw the lines of strain on his face, and realized how much effort it took for him not to climax right then.

"Oh, Jamie," she murmured, and pressed her mouth against his, drawing on his tongue and mating hers slickly with his.

With a deep sound of satisfaction, Jamie withdrew and then plunged into her, again and then again. Rachel bent her knees to bring him even deeper, pressing her heels into his lower back as she welcomed each powerful thrust, until the mounting sensations began to swirl and coalesce at her core.

Jamie made a raw sound of need, and gripped her hip as he pounded into her. Rachel clutched at him, unable to tear her gaze from his, until the mounting pressure finally exploded, and all her muscles contracted inward, squeezing around his rigid length as wave after wave of the most intense pleasure she'd ever known crashed over her.

Jamie gave a harsh cry and at the last instant, pulled out of her. Rachel watched as he emptied himself onto her stomach in thick, pearly streams, and his face contorted in an expression of intense pleasure. Then he eased himself down beside her, curling an arm over her as he nuzzled her neck, his breathing still uneven.

Rachel had never experienced anything so raw or intimate in her life. She turned her head to find Jamie watching her. She was filled with awe that she could have that kind of effect on any man, never mind one like Jamie. Reaching out, she traced a finger along the line of his jaw, feeling the rough stubble against her fingertip.

"I'm in love with you, Jamie Colter."

For a moment, he just stared at her, and then he rolled onto his back and pressed the heel of his palm against his eyes as he made a sound that was half-groan and half-laugh. When he finally turned to look at her again, Rachel was stunned to see his eyes were moist.

"Do you know how long I've waited to hear you say that?"

Rachel rose up on one elbow and tenderly traced the contours of his mouth. "A week, maybe two?" she teased, smiling.

"All my life, babe. Literally, all my life."

"Well, if you want me, I'm yours," she said, and bent her head down to kiss him. "Because I know now it's true. We belong together."

Chapter Eighteen

THEY MANAGED TO shower and get dressed and return to the kitchen just minutes before Dylan arrived with Rachel's parents. Jamie wouldn't have cared if they'd been caught in the act, but Rachel wanted to break the news in her own way, and he was feeling so supremely satisfied with everything in his life right now, he could give her that.

"You didn't hurt your leg, did you?" Rachel asked, as he opened two bottles of beer and handed one to her.

"Nope. I've never felt better," he assured her, and pulled her in for a long, slow kiss.

"Any nightmares?" she asked, searching his eyes.

"Only ones where you're not in my life," he said.

"I'm here, and I'm not leaving."

"The nightmares are getting less frequent," he acknowledged. "The doctor says they may never go away completely, but I'm learning to cope."

"You can always talk to me."

He tightened his arms around her. "Having you there when I wake up is the best medicine I could ask for." Releasing her, he cocked his head and listened for a moment.

"I think we have company."

Rachel smiled. "They're here. I'll get the salad started. If I know Dylan, he's probably starving."

Jamie made his way through the house just as the front door opened, and Diane McCafferty poked her head through. "Hello! Is anyone home?"

"In here, Mom!" Rachel called.

Diane opened the door wider, and Dylan entered the house, sporting two crutches and a brace on his leg that went from his ankle to his thigh. It wasn't a cast, but it immobilized his leg just as effectively.

"Hey, man," Jamie said, and couldn't help from grinning. "Welcome home. Glad to see you up and around."

Dylan gave Jamie a rueful smile, before reaching out to fist-bump him. "Yeah, well, we make quite a pair. Glad to see you got your cast off. How soon before you head back to your unit?"

Jamie shrugged. "I'm not sure. Right now it's all up in the air. How about you? What's your recovery time?"

Dylan shook his head. "I don't know. The doc says it could be as much as six months, but we'll see. Hey, I gotta sit down." He grimaced. "Surprisingly, the stitches in my abdomen bother me more than my knee."

"They took out your spleen, bro," Jamie said. "That has to hurt."

He followed Dylan onto the deck, and they both settled into a chaise and laid their crutches aside. Dylan tipped his head back and closed his eyes.

"Man, it feels good to be home," he said.

"Yeah, well let's hope you feel the same in six weeks," Jamie said. "Trust me, when you reach that point, even a trip to the proctologist sounds fun."

Dylan cracked an eyelid and grinned. "You're killing my chi, man."

"Maybe now is the time we could start our own extreme adventure business," Jamie said, thoughtfully stroking his chin. "We'll call it *Adventures for the Incapacitated.*"

Dylan laughed. "*Mountaineering for the Maimed and Mangled.*"

"*The Out-of-Action Experience.*"

"What are you two laughing at?" Rachel said, as she stepped onto the deck and handed them each a beer. Laurel followed her, and Jamie was glad to see Rachel's earlier animosity had completely vanished.

"Hey, Laurel," he said. "I'm glad you came over."

She pushed her glasses up on her nose, and her gaze slid to Dylan, where it lingered. "Yes, I came as soon as I saw Dylan get out of the car. How are you feeling, Dylan?"

He shrugged, seemingly oblivious to the way she devoured him with her eyes. "As well as can be expected. Thanks for taking care of Boomer. You're the best."

Laurel flushed with pleasure. "Of course. Any time, you know that." Abruptly, she turned away and took a hasty sip of the soda she carried.

"So what were you two talking about?" Rachel asked. "I heard something about being out of action?"

Jamie took Rachel's hand and tugged her down until she was sitting on the chaise with him. "Dylan and I used to talk about starting our own extreme adventure company, so we were deciding what we would call it, considering neither of us can hike a flight of stairs, never mind a mountain. We thought the *Out-of-Action Adventures* had a nice ring to it."

Dylan cleared his throat. "So is this thing between you two—" He gestured vaguely toward the two of them with one hand. "Is this official?"

Jamie looked at Rachel, and she gave him a smile that made his toes curl. "Yes," she said. "It's the real deal, so get used to it."

Dylan held his hand up, but his mouth curved in a smile. "Whatever. I know he's had a thing for you since we were kids, so I'm glad you've finally put him out of his misery."

"I think it's wonderful," Laurel said, turning back to them. She looked at Dylan. "I've always thought friends-to-lovers romances are the best kind. Don't you think so?"

Dylan shrugged. "I guess I've never thought about it. I can't think of any friends I've wanted to cross that line with."

Laurel's face fell and she turned away again, her shoulders hunched. She stood gazing at the scenery, but Jamie was pretty sure she didn't see any of it. He couldn't understand how Dylan could be so blind. Didn't he realize Laurel was completely head over heels for him? Or maybe he did know, and this was his way of deflecting her attention without having to outright reject her.

He cast around for something to say when Rachel's parents, Diane and John, stepped onto the deck. To his surprise, Rachel leaned back against him and drew his arm around her waist.

Diane's eyes widened slightly, but Jamie thought he saw a smile touch her mouth.

"We're together," Rachel said, looking at each of her parents in turn. "I know this probably comes as a surprise, but we discovered something over the last two weeks. We belong together."

Diane smiled broadly. "Well, I'd be lying if I said I hadn't hoped this might happen. I'm very happy, for both of you!"

Rachel's father cleared his throat, and looked uncomfortable. "You're both adults. You certainly don't need our permission, but I will say I'm glad you finally unloaded that worthless piece of crap you called a husband, and found yourself a good man." Leaning forward, he shook Jamie's hand. "I guess this means we'll be seeing more of you, son."

Dylan snorted. "As if he didn't practically live at our house growing up."

Jamie laughed and tightened his arm around Rachel. "See?" he said, looking at her. "I told you it was meant to be."

The tension went out of Rachel's body and she gave him

a brilliant smile and curled her hand over his. "You were right." She narrowed her eyes at him. "So what is this about starting your own adventure company?"

Jamie looked over at Dylan. "We've always talked about starting our own business, but then we went our separate ways and it never materialized."

"But if I can't jump again—" Dylan began.

"And if the Marines won't let me rejoin my unit," Jamie said, "then that's something we could consider doing, instead."

"Hmm," Diane mused. "What kinds of adventures would you offer?"

"Well, there're plenty of options right here in Montana," Dylan said. "Rock climbing, parasailing, white water rafting, snowboarding, and that sort of thing."

Rachel considered for a moment. "If you're really serious, then you should consider going even more extreme." At their questioning looks, she smiled. "I'd offer scuba diving on the Great Barrier Reef, or heli-skiing in Canada, and mountain biking in the Alps."

There was a momentary silence as they each considered what she said.

"That sounds great," Dylan finally replied, "but who would handle the logistics? We'd need hotels, and equipment, and guides, and—" He broke off as Jamie gave him a meaningful look. "Ah. Of course. Rachel could do all of that."

"I could," Rachel agreed. "I may not be part of Elite

Concierge Services anymore, but I still have connections. I'd love to help you plan some adventures."

"We'll need an office, and staff members," Jamie said. "And all of that requires capital. I have some money set aside we could use, but I doubt it will be enough."

Rachel shifted to look at him. "I think I can help with that. You see, I have this car I'm trying to sell—"

"Not the Porsche!" Jamie protested.

Rachel laughed. "Yes, the Porsche. You don't really want me to keep it, do you?"

"Not if it reminds you of Deke in any way," he grudgingly admitted. "In fact, I kind of like the idea of that bastard's money underwriting our business venture."

Rachel laughed. "Then count me in. If it means keeping you here in Glacier Creek, then I'm all for it."

"This calls for a toast," Diane said, smiling. She raised her glass of wine, and the others joined in. "To the start of a wonderful partnership—" she looked meaningfully at Rachel and Jamie "—both professionally and personally."

Rachel turned and, as everyone cheered, cupped Jamie's face in her hands and kissed him sweetly. "I love you, Jamie Colter," she said softly. "Here's to a lifelong partnership."

Jamie's expression was tender as his gaze traveled over her face. "Oh, the adventures we're going to have, Rachel."

As everyone looked on, smiling their approval, he kissed her.

The End

The Glacier Creek Series

Book 1: *A Hot Montana Summer*

Book 2: *The Firefighter's Slow Burn*

Book 3: Coming soon

Available now at your favorite online retailer!

About the Author

Karen Foley admits to being an incurable romantic. When she's not working for the Department of Defense, she loves writing sexy stories about alpha heroes and strong heroines. Karen lives in New England with her husband, two daughters, and a houseful of pets.

Thank you for reading

A Hot Montana Summer

If you enjoyed this book, you can find more from all our great authors at TulePublishing.com, or from your favorite online retailer.

Made in the USA
Columbia, SC
25 April 2018